THE FIANCÉ IS FINISHED

A HUMOROUS PARANORMAL COZY MYSTERY

CARLY WINTER

Edited by
DIVAS AT WORK EDITING
Cover by
COVEREDBYMELINDA.COM

WESTWARD PUBLISHING / CARLY FALL, LLC

THE FIANCÉ IS FINISHED

Did he die because of money, love or revenge?

When a man is found dead in a hotel room, Bernie's friend, Darla, becomes one of the main suspects. With her fragile mental health on the line, she begs Bernie to find the real killer to save her from spiraling into a dark episode.

Bernie and Deputy Adam Gallagher have been an item for months, but when she questions him about the murder, she finds him unwilling to give her the information she needs to ease Darla's concerns.

To find the true killer, Bernie is forced to make a decision that could ruin her relationship with Adam... if she's caught. With her ghostly grandmother's help, she puts everything on the line to find the murderer.

CHAPTER 1

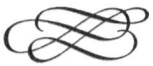

"Clean and worry, clean and worry. You'll get old in a hurry." Ruby, the ghost of my dead grandmother, chided as she trailed behind me up the stairs of our home. "Let's go do something fun!"

"I need to make a living," I replied. "Pay bills, put food on the table... little things like that."

Business had been brisk at my bed and breakfast, but that meant I had to bust my bottom. For the past two weeks I'd had every room rented out and I had no idea why. I hadn't even had time to research what had brought everyone to Sedona—

perhaps a golf tournament or a spiritual guru event. The flood of reservations had finally stopped, giving me the chance to breathe a bit. Over the next couple of days, I planned to do some hiking, spend some time with my boyfriend, Adam, and read a few books.

But first, I had to get the guest rooms cleaned.

"I shouldn't have spent so much of my money while alive," Ruby muttered. "If I'd known I was going to be a ghost after death trapped with my workaholic granddaughter, I would have saved more cash to leave to you so we could go have some fun."

"No one wishes that more than me," I said, opening the door to the first guest room. After a cursory glance, I sighed with relief. A tidy customer always made my job a little easier.

Ruby had willed me the fabulous house, the ATV and a few thousand dollars. More importantly, she'd given me the opportunity to leave Louisiana and start a fresh life in Sedona, Arizona, a place I loved. It hadn't always been easy making ends meet, but I did pretty well with the bed and breakfast. It was a lot of work, though.

"Well, who could have predicted we'd be in this pickle, right?" Ruby asked.

Turning to my ghostly grandmother, I nodded. "Never in a million years would I have thought we'd find ourselves in this situation."

I loved Ruby, but we were so different. While I tended to be a bit uptight about... well, everything, I doubted she'd ever experienced one moment of stress. She had lived life on her own terms, and she tried to get me to do the same. But I wasn't wired that way. I needed order, while she preferred chaos. I liked my life quiet, but for her, the more going on the better. She'd never said it, but I think she found *me* a little boring, not just my life. Her being stuck on this plane was trying at times. But other times, I appreciated her levity and her reminding me to relax and cut loose a bit.

However, that wouldn't be happening today. I'd never be able to rest until the rooms were cleaned. Just knowing there was a mess in the house made me uneasy.

I began with the bed and stripped the sheets and vacuumed the mattress. Once it was made and I'd arranged the pillows, Ruby settled in on the comforter to watch me. In her state, she couldn't exactly help because she couldn't move inanimate objects. Unfortunately, a toilet scrub brush would never find its way into her hand.

After finishing the room except for the vacuuming, I moved across the hall and opened the door. In a deep, ominous voice, Ruby said, "Duh, duh, duh... the Death Room."

A drug trafficker had died in the room a while back, and she never let me forget it. "Would you please stop saying that?"

Ruby cackled and brushed past me inside, causing a chill to crawl over my skin. "Nope. Never going to happen. Now, hurry up so we can move on to something exciting."

I may have uttered a few curses as I scrubbed the bathroom. When the sound of the front door chimes filtered up from the first floor, I whispered a slew of naughty words and checked my phone to see if someone had made a reservation. Nothing.

Which meant the person downstairs was a walk-in, or a salesperson had arrived. I wasn't expecting any friends so I hoped for a salesperson because I hated walk-ins. They always tried to talk me down on my pricing.

"I'll go see who it is!" Ruby yelled as she raced down the hallway, obviously excited about the intrusion.

With a sigh, I straightened my ponytail and ran a hand over my *Breakfast Club* T-shirt. I loved the movies from the eighties and had the T-shirt collection to prove it.

After grabbing a towel, I wiped the sweat dotting my forehead. Purple bags hung under my eyes, showing the strain I'd been under the past two weeks.

"That's as good as it's going to get," I muttered to my reflection in the mirror, then headed downstairs.

"Where do we know this one from?" Ruby asked as I entered the foyer. She circled my guest with her arms crossed over her chest.

A familiar face stood at my door, but like Ruby, I couldn't place the name.

"Hi, Bernie," the woman said, her smile sad. "Do you remember me?"

I grinned and wracked my memory. I knew this woman with the long blonde hair, although there was something different about her. Yet, I couldn't place her name to save my life. I quickly recalled all the stores I'd visited in town thinking she'd clerked there. Or maybe a friend of Darla's I'd seen at the diner?

"I do," I replied. There was only so long I could stare at someone before things became awkward and uncomfortable. "But where and how escapes me. And I can't remember your name, either."

"I'm Amy," she said. "My friend Cathy and I stayed here a few months back while I was looking for a place to get married."

Of course! Amy, the exuberant one; her friend Cathy, the quiet sidekick. "Oh, wow! Come in! What can I do for you?"

She followed me into the living room

dragging her suitcase behind her and smiled as she glanced around. "I'm sorry I didn't make a reservation. It was a last-minute trip. Do you have a room for me?"

"I think so. How long will you be staying?" I asked.

"I'm... I'm not sure," she said, sinking onto the couch. "A few days. I had to get out of Phoenix. Your place is so homey and welcoming, I drove up here on a whim."

"What do you think she's running from?" Ruby asked, tapping her chin with her forefinger. "Maybe she killed someone? That's what we need! Another murder investigation!"

My chest swelled with pride as I ignored Ruby. Amy had chosen my place and driven two hours to stay. I must have made quite the impression on her.

"No problem," I said. "I'm just finishing up the cleaning on one room. Are you okay waiting for a few minutes?"

"Sure. Of course."

"I'll be back in a little bit," I said as her phone began to ring.

She stared at the device as tears welled

in her eyes. Obviously, something was up-setting her, and it wasn't my place to poke my nose into her business.

But apparently, Ruby had other plans as she settled in right next to the woman and studied her carefully.

"Hello?" Amy said just as I arrived at the top of the stairs. I quickly vacuumed the first room I'd cleaned and out in the hall-way. After doing a final check to make sure nothing in the space caught my critical eye, I was comfortable getting Amy checked in. My online reviews always mentioned how clean my place was, and I didn't want to dis-appoint.

Ruby appeared in the doorway just as I was about to head downstairs. "Shut the door!" she yelled. "Hurry up! Shut it!"

I quietly closed the panel and turned to my hysterical ghost. "What's going on?"

"The drama llama has arrived!" she squealed with glee.

"The drama llama?"

"Yes! Blondie downstairs is hauling around not only her clothes in that suitcase, but more drama and emotional baggage than you can imagine!"

I really wanted to ignore Ruby, but I'd also wondered what Amy's story was. Why show up at my place by herself, completely unannounced looking sadder than a Bassett Hound? "What's going on?"

"Remember when she was here before and looking for a place to get married? With Chatty Cathy, and I say that with every ounce of sarcasm I can muster?"

I rolled my eyes. "Yes."

"Well, her fiancé called when you came upstairs. Apparently, they've broken up because he's a no good, two-timing, cheating horse's behind."

"Oh, that's too bad," I muttered. "I feel awful for her." I tried to imagine what it would be like finding out my boyfriend, Adam, had been with another woman, and bile rose in my throat. We weren't anywhere close to marriage, so the pain must be tenfold for Amy.

"The fiancé, who we'll refer to as Cunning Colin from now on, is on his way up to Sedona to win her back."

"Here?" I asked, pointing at the carpeted floor. "He's coming here?"

"Not here, as in this house. She told him to check into Sedona Grand Hotel and she's going to see him later this afternoon."

"Thank goodness," I whispered, having visions of the two of them fighting in the living room and me trying to stay out of the way. Ruby, of course, would insert herself into the melee and cheer one of them on.

"This is our chance!" she whispered as she rubbed her hands together, her gaze gleaming with mischief. "I have a great plan."

"I hate it when you say that," I replied. "It always means trouble for me."

"No! Just listen. We'll go to the hotel and follow Amy to Cunning Colin's room. I'll sneak in and spy on them and I can keep you updated on the drama while you wait in the hallway."

As Ruby did a little jig, I crossed my arms over my chest. "Absolutely not. Have you forgotten what happened the last time we pulled that stunt? I was almost dropped down a stairwell to my death. We're minding our own business."

Ruby's face fell. "I love you dearly, but this business of yours is boring, Bernie. Come on and humor your dead granny. Let's get out and chase some excitement."

"We will," I said. "I've just been so busy with the bed and breakfast, I haven't had time to do anything but work."

"So let's go spy on the drama llama and find out what Cunning Colin has to say for himself!"

"No, Ruby. I'm not sticking my nose where it doesn't belong because you're bored."

She narrowed her gaze at me while pouting like a two-year-old. "Fine."

"Now, I'm going to get Amy checked in and then I'm going to finish cleaning the last room."

Ruby glared at me but remained quiet. As I turned to head back downstairs, admittedly, I was curious about why Amy had traveled all the way to Sedona after breaking up with her fiancé. In her state of heartbreak, perhaps she needed as much space as possible from him.

I smiled as I entered the living room. Amy was still sitting on the couch, wiping her cheeks.

"Are you okay?" I asked. "Is there anything I can do for you?"

She shook her head. "I broke up with my fiancé because I caught him cheating on me. For some reason, I found myself throwing clothes in a bag and heading to Sedona."

"I'm really sorry to hear that, Amy," I replied as I moved behind the desk and pulled out the iPad to start the check-in process.

"He's coming up to Sedona, but I told him he can't come here," she said. "I figured you didn't need to be caught in the middle of this mess."

I smiled, grateful she'd be keeping me out of it.

"He's staying at a hotel and wants to talk with me this afternoon." As she spoke, she typed her information into the iPad. "He says he wants to win me back."

"Do you think it'll work?" I asked. "Do you want him back?"

She sighed and stared at me a long moment as more tears tracked down her cheeks. After swiping at them, she replied, "I don't know, Bernie. Right now, I'm so angry and hurt, I just want to kill him."

CHAPTER 2

"Well, I'd rather go spy on the drama llama than visit Adam and his unfriendly ghost, but at least we're getting out of the house," Ruby said as we strolled down the sidewalk.

Adam and I hadn't had much time to spend together the past couple of weeks and I looked forward to us going on a hike. Despite her hatred of hiking, Ruby had insisted she come. Secretly, I thought she wanted to speak with Adam's ghost, Ned, but I'd never question her on it. She'd only deny it but I could see that he intrigued her, just as he did me. A guy who had died hundreds of years ago from a bullet through his chest? Both of us were curious about the details he'd yet to share whether Ruby would admit it or not.

"Hey!" Adam greeted when he answered the door and took me into a warm embrace. "I've missed you!"

"Same here!" I glanced over his shoulder. Ruby had invited herself in and stood in the living room yelling for Ned.

"I think I smelled Ruby walk by," Adam whispered.

"You did. She's trying to get Ned to show himself." Ruby's distinct scent of lavender and marijuana was often hard to ignore. He couldn't see or hear her—no one could but me—and sometimes I wondered what I must have done in a past life to be struck by lightning and suddenly possess the ability to see ghosts.

Adam shut the door and turned in Ruby's direction. "What's the deal? Don't I even get a hello anymore?"

She glanced over at him then at me. "Is he talking to me?"

I nodded. Adam had begun speaking directly to my ghost a while back, and it only endeared him to me more.

With a grin, she sauntered over to Adam and stood right in front of him. "Tell the copper I say hello and he's got nice legs."

Adam wore a pair of denim shorts, and yes, his legs looked great, but I wasn't going to tell him that. "Ruby says hi."

"I smell her. She's right here in front of me, but for some reason I have a feeling she's saying more than hello."

Ruby cackled and turned away. "Where's Nutjob Ned?"

As if on cue, the ghost appeared in the living room on the other side of the couch, probably wanting a barrier between him and Ruby.

"There you are!" Ruby said as she strode toward him. "I was wondering when you'd come out and say howdy."

Ned glanced over at me and smiled. "Miss Bernadette."

I'd told him at least a dozen times he didn't need to address me that way, but he didn't seem to be able to stop. Old habits didn't die easily for dead men.

I grinned as Ruby rounded the couch toward him. "Nice to see you again, Ned," she said.

"Not quite sure yet if I can say the same, ma'am."

"You don't need to call me that," Ruby said, waving her hand in front of her face.

"I like to respect my elders."

With a snort, I turned away so Ruby wouldn't see the fits of giggles threatening to explode from me.

"I'm not your elder, Ned. I died just over three years ago. From what little I know about you, you've got me beat in the dead department by decades, if not centuries."

Once I'd gained control of myself again, I watched the two. Ruby seemed to be attempting to get on Ned's good side.

"What do you say us two ghosts learn something about each other?" Ruby asked.

"Ma'am—I mean Ruby—I'm not sure I've ever met anyone quite like you, and frankly, you scare me a little bit."

"Scare you?"

"Yes. I've considered that perhaps you

have a little Satan in your heart, and I'm not sure what to make of that."

Now it was Ruby's turn to laugh. "Relax, Old Timer," she replied. "I'm as harmless as a hummingbird, especially in my current state. I may run my mouth a lot, but that's about it."

"Well, I suppose we could make a go at being friendly," Ned said, his voice full of hesitation.

"Excellent. Now tell me how you bit the big one. I want details."

Adam whispered, 'What's going on? I'm missing out on something, right?"

I nodded and brought my finger to my lips signaling him to be quiet, not wanting to miss a word.

"Bit the big one?" Ned asked, his brow furrowed in confusion. "I didn't bite anyone."

Ruby threw her head back and laughed. "I meant, how did you die?"

"Oh! Well, I was a bank robber and—"

"A bank robber!" Ruby yelled. "This is so exciting. Tell me everything!"

Ned glanced over Ruby's shoulder at me,

as if looking for permission to tell his tale. I nodded, just as interested as Ruby.

"It was 1899, the same year the San Francisco Chronicle called the town of Jerome, Arizona the wickedest town in America. My partner and I, a good fella named Sam, decided to visit the place. Now, Sam was always on the hunt for the next score, and we believed we found it in Jerome."

"The bank," Ruby said.

"Yes, ma'am."

"Ruby. Call me Ruby."

"My apologies. Yes, the bank. We stayed in town a couple of days and got the lay of the land. Studied the habits of the bank workers and the sheriff. Who opened the bank, who closed it. What the sheriff did all day. Things like that."

"Smart." Ruby nodded as though she plotted bank robberies every day. "Very smart."

"We realized the lawman went to the brothel every day at noon, so we figured that was our time to hit the bank."

"Good thinking," she agreed.

"Well, it turned out it wasn't," Ned said. "We went into the bank, held everyone up and got our money. While we were riding out of town on our horses, the sheriff and a deputy of his stopped us. Sam had the guts to ask why the sheriff wasn't in the brothel, and he said his favorite girl didn't work on Wednesdays."

"That is simply horrible luck," Ruby said, shaking her head. "Absolutely horrible."

"Agreed. But old Sam, he decided he wasn't going down without a fight." Ned pointed to his bloodstained chest. "We lost."

"If you died in Jerome, why are you in Sedona?" I asked.

"Miss Bernadette, I didn't die in Jerome. After being shot, I was able to stay on my horse and rode out of town. Found myself in a barn taking my last breaths, and here I am today."

I glanced around the condo trying to picture it as a barn. When the barn had been flattened, what had been built before the condo had been erected? How many cycles of tear downs had occurred over the hundreds of years? The world was always in such a state of flux. It may come slowly and it may take years, but change was inevitable.

"And you've been trapped in every building since then?" I asked.

He nodded, but his focus remained on Ruby. "And how did you die?"

I cringed as she explained. "Well, I was in bed with my handyman for a little romp between the sheets. I'd just gotten up to fetch us some beers and my ticker gave out."

Ned arched an eyebrow but didn't comment.

"What's going on?" Adam whispered.

"Ned used to be a bank robber," I replied. "He died in a barn and has been trapped in the buildings since."

"Oh, wow. A bank robber living with a cop. That seems wrong on a lot of different levels."

"I agree," I mumbled.

"These two are going for a hike today," Ruby said as she hitched her thumb over her shoulder at Adam and me. "Do you want to see if you can leave this place?"

Ned glanced over at me then shrugged.

"I'm very happy here by myself. I like the quiet."

Which was a good thing because there was absolutely no proof that the ghost could leave the condo. Throughout the years he'd tried but hadn't been successful.

"But Bernie over there has some magical powers," Ruby said. "She got hit by lightning and now she sees me. I can leave my place where I was trapped, as long as I'm with her. Maybe it'll be the same for you, Ned."

"And we don't know why that happens," I interjected, not wanting Ned to get his hopes up. "We don't know why I can see you or why you can leave the house with me, but not by yourself."

"That's true," Ruby replied. "We really don't know diddly-squat about why things are the way they are. But that doesn't mean we can't give it a try."

Yes, I was curious if I'd be able to release Ned from the condo, but in a way, I also hoped I couldn't because that would make me some type of ghost Pied Piper. Nope. I didn't want to run around collecting the spirits of the dead.

"Let's give it a try, anyway," Ruby encouraged.

"I think we're ready to leave," I said, turning to Adam. "Ruby wants Ned to come with us."

"Can he?"

"We're about to find out."

I opened the door and stepped outside. Adam and Ruby followed. Ned stood on the threshold and stared out at us, seemingly hesitant to take his first step.

"Come on." Ruby waved at him. "It's not like you're walking into a pit of vipers."

Or maybe that's how he perceived it. A lot had changed since 1899. Mainly, cars whizzed by on paved roads. Most people rode their horses in more deserted areas. Not to mention the leaps and bounds in technology that had taken place.

One boot crossed the threshold, then the other. A slow smile spread over his face. "Well, I'll be darned."

"Woohoo!" Ruby hooted. "Let's go see the world, Ned!"

I grinned at Adam. "Apparently, I'm

some type of ghost wrangler," I muttered. "He's free and coming with us."

His eyes widened and he shook his head. "Unbelievable. I wonder why you can do this."

"You and me both." I didn't try to think too hard on why I could free ghosts from their eternal confines. Instead, I focused on enjoying the day with my boyfriend. He took my hand in his, and we walked down the path.

"Is it a warm day?" Ned asked. "It seems like it would be warm."

I glanced up at the blue skies. "Fall is right around the corner, so there's a bit of a chill in the air."

"Ah, I loved this time of year while alive," Ruby said with a sigh. "Actually, I loved every day. Every single one of them was perfect, even when it wasn't."

"We can catch a trailhead right up here." Adam pointed down the road a bit. "It's a quick mile loop."

"That sounds perfect."

Glancing over my shoulder, I noted Ruby and Ned walking side by side about ten feet behind us. With his size, he dwarfed my grandmother. The distinct differences in time caught at the moments of their deaths wasn't lost on me: Ned from another era in his cowboy dress, Ruby in her purple mumu.

Ned's head swiveled all around as he took in the modern world, his eyes wide in amazement. Despite my reservations about being a ghost herder, I was happy to give him a new freedom, to have him witness how we lived outside of his confines.

Ruby was tethered to me by about fifteen feet, but was Ned?

"Could you stop right there?" I asked, holding up my hand to them. I kept walking. Both were snapped back within the fifteen-foot unseen leash.

"What's going on?" Adam asked.

"I wanted to see if Ned was tied to me like Ruby is when we're out and about."

"And is he?"

"Yes."

We continued on our way. Ned and Ruby talked in low tones and I couldn't decipher what they said, which was fine with me. As long as they weren't arguing as they had in the past, I didn't care what they discussed.

A few moments later, Ruby yelled, "Hey, Bernie! Watch this!"

I turned to find her and Ned in the road, a car speeding right at them.

With a gasp, I brought my hand to my mouth. My first instinct was to run out into the lane and push them both aside, but they jumped out of the way at the last second. As I tried to calm my thundering heart, I leaned over and placed my hands on my knees.

"We got you with that one!" Ruby yelled.

"What's wrong?" Adam asked. "Are you feeling okay?"

Ruby and Ned laughed like they'd just pulled off the funniest joke ever. When I was sure I wasn't going to have a heart attack, I watched them again.

"They're playing chicken with the cars," I said as another one sped by and the ghosts sprang out of the way, both in hysterics.

"I suppose it doesn't matter since they're both dead, right?" Adam asked with a chuckle. "But I can understand how you'd be upset watching their antics."

The two continued their silly game and I was finally able to relax a bit. Although Ned had seemed a little quiet and introverted at first, Ruby had brought out a different side to him. He was having just as much fun.

However, I could barely handle Ruby and her adventures. Add Ned and his seemingly carefree attitude into the mix... was that a good thing, or was my life about to become infinitely more difficult?

CHAPTER 3

he next morning as I was oiling the staircase banister, the chimes on the front door rang, indicating someone had entered. I hurried down the stairs and Ruby appeared at the bottom of them. She loved when we had visitors.

"It's that other girl," she said, disappointment in her voice. "The one who doesn't talk much."

When I reached the bottom of the staircase, I glanced up to find Cathy, Amy's friend, standing by the front door. A stunning woman, she wore her black hair in a pixie cut and she possessed the bluest eyes I'd ever seen. However, I also noted deep, purple circles hung under them, making her look absolutely exhausted.

"Hi," she greeted me. "Do you remember me?"

"Of course, Cathy," I replied. "Amy told me you'd be coming. It's nice to see you again."

She nodded and followed me over to the check-in desk. I remembered her being somewhat quiet, but as the silence stretched while she filled out the reservation form on the iPad, it became uncomfortable. I found myself chewing on my nails and trying not to say something to make the situation even more awkward.

"How is she?" Cathy finally asked as she handed me back the device.

"Amy? I'm not sure. I haven't seen her since yesterday."

Cathy nodded. "That guy is such a jerk. I hope she doesn't go back with him. Did she tell you this is the third time I know of that he's been caught cheating?"

I shook my head. "Uh… no."

"Why he ever asked her to marry him in the first place, I have no idea."

I reached for her room key and handed it to her. "Here you go. Same room as last time you were here," I said with a smile, hoping she'd head upstairs and end the unpleasant conversation.

"Thanks. Is Amy also in the same room as last time?"

"Yes. I'm not sure if she's here though. Like I said, I haven't seen her since yesterday."

"She's probably asleep," Cathy muttered. "The last time he did this, I couldn't get her out of bed for a week."

"More drama, Bernie," Ruby said as she strode up next to Cathy. "More drama. This is going to get interesting. I can tell."

I didn't want to be involved in any of it, so I just smiled.

"He had the audacity to come up here and try to win her back," Cathy continued. "Did she tell you that?"

"Yes. I understand they spoke yesterday."

"Have you seen her since?"

"No, I haven't. I was out all day yesterday. I didn't return until after dark."

Why did I feel the need to give Cathy details of my comings and goings?

"I was supposed to come up yesterday as well," she explained. "I couldn't find anyone to cover my shift, so I got up before dawn to make the drive up here."

"You're a good friend," I murmured, unsure of what I was supposed to say to her.

"I'm exhausted," she muttered. "I'm sorry if I'm being short and cranky. Amy and Colin... that's her fiancé... there's always something going on between them. I'm the one picking up the pieces of Amy's self-esteem after he destroys it."

Frankly, it didn't sound like a friendship I'd want to be involved with, but to each their own.

"Ask Cathy if Amy caught him in bed with someone," Ruby said. "If not, how did she know he was cheating? I want all the gory details!"

Yeah, I wasn't going to go there. I didn't want any more information. The less I knew about the mess, the better off I'd be. "Well, I hope everything gets worked out," I said.

"Me too," Cathy replied, sighing. "I'll head upstairs and take a quick nap before knocking on Amy's door. She's so awful if you wake her when she's sleeping."

"Sounds good. We aren't expecting anyone else, so the house should remain quiet."

As Cathy lugged her suitcase up the stairs, Ruby came to stand in front of me. "I feel like she needs to be haunted."

"Please just leave them be. We want Amy to figure out what she's going to do with the boyfriend and then leave. We don't need the drama."

"Sure we do!" Ruby exclaimed. "What's life without comedies and tragedies? It's boring, that's what. I hope he shows up here. I want to see a knockout war of words. I'd also like to get a look at him and see what's so special that Amy's gone back to him after he's cheated on her. I certainly wouldn't put up with that."

Of course she wouldn't. But I sometimes wondered if Ruby had truly become emotionally invested in anyone in her life.

Would I go back to Adam if I found out

he had slept with another woman? I'd like to think not. However, love did funny things to a person.

But back to oiling the banister. Living in Arizona, the wood had to be constantly taken care of or it began to crack. The last thing I needed was a guest with a wayward splinter courtesy of my staircase railing.

A few moments later, another knock sounded at the front door.

"I hope this is Cunning Colin!" Ruby shouted as she appeared in the living room.

Praying that it wasn't, relief swept through me as I opened the door. Darla.

"Gosh dang it!" Ruby yelled. "I wanted it to be Colin, not her!"

Then go away.

It wasn't until a couple of months ago that I found out Darla suffered from schizophrenia. She'd actually gone off her medicine for a period of time and it had led to behavioral changes that had caused a huge wedge in our friendship. Thankfully, we were repairing our relationship but that didn't mean I felt comfortable talking to my ghost in front of her. Darla had enough on her plate without trying to understand my paranormal secrets.

"Hey!" I said, smiling, until I realized my friend had tears rolling down her face and she trembled from head to toe.

"Darla, what's wrong?" I said, taking her hand and pulling her inside to the couches. Once we sat down, she couldn't meet my gaze, but she continued to cry as she tucked her blonde hair behind her ears. Ruby was nowhere to be found, which was fine by me. Trying to have a conversation with someone while she was always offering her opinion was difficult at best.

"Take some deep breaths," I coaxed, gently laying my hand on Darla's shoulder.

She stared off into space and breathed in and out, long and slow. After a moment, she turned to me. "I'm in trouble."

"Tell me what's the matter." I gave her what I hoped was a reassuring half-smile.

"I need your help, Bernie," she said, gripping my hand with such force, I thought she may snap my fingers. "Please tell me you'll help me."

Dread filled me at her tone. "You know I

will, Darla. What's wrong?!"

"I went to open the diner this morning."

Staring at her expectantly, I waited for her to state the horrible, awful thing she wanted me to help her with. A spider? The cooler had gone down? A plugged-up dishwasher? She ran out of ketchup?

"And the police were there," she said.

"What did they want?"

"To question me about a murder."

My stomach dropped. A murder?

"I didn't do it, Bernie! I swear to you, I didn't!"

"Do the police think you did?"

"They said I was a suspect," she continued, tears streaming down her face.

Oh, no.

"Did someone say murder?" Ruby asked, sitting next to my friend. "Now things are getting interesting around here."

I shot Ruby a glare. "Tell me what they said, Darla. Try to relax and recall the conversation. Start at the beginning."

She took a few more deep breaths and closed her eyes for a long moment. When she met my gaze again, she had calmed a bit.

"There was a murder at the Sedona Grand Hotel last night," she began. "Some guy was stabbed in his hotel room."

I furrowed my brow, utterly confused. "What does that have to do with you?"

"The police found a takeout bag from my diner in his room, so they came to question me."

"That doesn't mean they think you committed the murder," I said, my anxiety slowly ebbing. "They're covering their bases."

She shook her head. "No, Bernie. They showed me a picture of the guy and I had a bad experience with him when he came in the prior night. I was apparently one of the last people to see him alive."

"That doesn't mean you killed him."

"They think it does."

Uncertain if it was the paranoia brought on by her mental illness or if she truly had something to fear, I decided to probe a little further.

"Darla, why would they think you killed him? Tell me what happened when you saw him."

She glanced around the living room, still gripping my hand with force. "He came in late last night, just as I was about to turn out the lights, and asked for a milkshake and a club sandwich to go. I told him the kitchen was closed. He didn't appreciate my answer and started throwing a hissy fit."

"What did he say?"

"He yelled that he wanted something during his trip to go right in this dumpy town and if I could please give him a sandwich, he'd appreciate it. He said it a little more colorfully, though. Lots of swearing."

"Why didn't you call the police?"

Darla shrugged. "I did, but later. It seemed easier to just get the jerk his food than to deal with the cops."

I tried to put myself in Darla's shoes, and I understood. If she'd called the police, she'd most likely have to file reports and be interviewed. Getting the jerk what he wanted and sending him on his way was the path of least resistance. "What happened then?"

"He not only stiffed me, he called me a cow and broke a chair on his way out for good measure. Then he told me he was staying at the Sedona Grand Hotel if I wanted to try to collect from him."

"Are you kidding me?!"

"No. His behavior was awful."

"What happened then?"

"That's when I called the cops—after he left. They came and took my statement, but I didn't know anything about him." She stared at the floor for a long moment. "I was so angry, Bernie, and I let the police know it. I totally lost my cool. I called him a bunch of names and ended up throwing a glass at the wall... all in front of Sheriff Walker."

"I can't imagine this girl even raising her voice," Ruby cut in. "She's got a little fire in her I wasn't aware of."

"Did you have to go down to the station or anything?" I asked, equally surprised by Darla's outburst.

She shook her head. "No. Walker took my statement and then I went upstairs to bed."

Darla lived in a cozy apartment above the diner that perpetually smelled of bacon and roses, a very strange combination I found quite pleasant.

"Then the police showed up at your restaurant this morning?" I asked.

"Yes. They told me that the man from last night had been murdered with a knife. They asked me a bunch of questions about it and referred to how angry I'd been the night before. They were very interested in my knife sets."

As I stared at my friend, my anxiety rose once again because I could see why the sheriff was interested in her. First, she'd had a very unpleasant run-in with the victim. He'd stiffed her, and she'd been furious. She also owned a restaurant, so there were knives all over the place.

"Did... did you see or talk to anyone last night after the police left?" I asked, hoping she'd called her mom or another friend.

Darla shook her head. "I went upstairs and watched a rerun of *Friends*, then the late-night news. I fell asleep on the couch."

Uh-oh. Darla didn't have an alibi either.

The knock at the front door startled us both. I hurried over and caught a glimpse of the police cruiser sitting outside through the window.

"Just a minute!" I called, then hurried back to Darla. "The cops are here," I whispered.

"Oh, my gosh!" she said, jumping to her feet. "I need to leave! I can't deal with them right now!"

"Go out the back door," I hissed. "I'll call you later."

She grabbed my hands once again as tears streamed down her face, complete desperation in her gaze. "Bernie, please find the killer. Please. I… I can't deal with this. I can't go to jail. I can't handle any of it. Some days I feel like I'm barely getting by. This will break me."

I nodded and pushed her toward the kitchen. "Go, Darla. I'll be in touch."

I waited until I heard the back door click shut, then took a few deep breaths, hoping the cruiser out front meant Adam had come to say hello and not something having to do with the murdered man at the hotel.

"That was weird," Ruby said. "If she didn't have anything to do with that dead guy, why is she running from the police?"

An excellent question.

CHAPTER 4

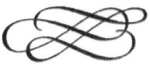

$\mathcal{I}$ opened the door to find Adam staring at me grimly.

"What's up?" I asked as dread settled in my gut. If he had stopped by to say hello, he'd be smiling. Instead, he had on what I had recently dubbed his "cop face." All business and very serious.

"I'm looking for Amy Parsons."

Well, that threw me for a loop. What in the heck did he want with Amy? I had expected him to somehow know Darla was here and ask for her. "What for?"

He rolled his eyes. "Bernie, I need to speak with her immediately. It's police business."

What had Amy done?

"Come on in," I said, stepping aside. "I think she's upstairs."

"Which room?"

"First on the left. Can I ask what's going on?"

He strode into the living room and glanced upstairs, then turned to me. "A gentleman named Colin Victory was murdered last night. Her name was found in his phone and on a piece of paper along with your address on the hotel room desk. I took a stab and guessed she was staying here."

Ruby appeared right in front of Adam. "Colin? As in Cunning Colin? The guy Amy was going to marry?"

Adam stepped back. "I can smell Ruby, but I'm not in the mood for any of her games. I've got another murder to solve."

"Someone's a little cranky," Ruby muttered.

Suddenly, the murder had hit very close to home. "Adam, what do you need me to do?" I asked.

"I'm going upstairs and I'd like to do a quick interview with Amy here in the living room. A little privacy and none of Ruby's antics would be nice."

"Will do," I said.

Without another word, he headed upstairs and knocked on Amy's door. After waiting a moment, he tapped again.

As their muffled conversation filtered to the living room, Ruby and I both stared up at the landing. A few seconds later, Adam descended with Amy trailing behind him.

She glanced over at me, her brow furrowed in confusion. Dressed in black sweats and an oversized red sweatshirt, her blonde hair lay in tangles around her shoulders. She'd obviously been sleeping.

"Please sit, Ms. Parsons," Adam ordered, pointing at the sofa.

"I'll be in the bedroom," I muttered as he shot me a glare, indicating he wanted me to disappear.

"This is your house," Ruby said. "You have every right to know what's going on here."

"I told Adam I'd leave him alone," I whispered once we were in the kitchen.

"Fine. You do that, but I'm going to listen."

I stood at my door and grit my teeth. Ruby was correct. I had every right to know what was going on with Amy. If Adam wanted privacy, he should have taken her down to the police station.

I opened and closed the door as if I'd done what he asked and gone to my bedroom. Then I dropped to my knees and crawled into the kitchen to hide behind the island. Past eavesdropping attempts had proven the spot to be an excellent location.

"Ms. Parsons, do you know someone named Colin Victory?" Adam asked.

"Yes. He's... he was my fiancé."

"*Was* your fiancé?"

"Yes. I broke up with him. I found out he was cheating on me."

"When was the last time you saw him?" Adam asked. Although I couldn't see into the room, I imagined him jotting down everything she said in his notebook.

"Last night," Amy replied. "Why? What's going on? Has he done something?"

Adam sighed. "He's dead, Ms. Parsons."

An oppressive, heavy moment of silence blanketed the room while Amy processed what Adam had shared. The pain-filled, glass-shattering scream from her startled me so badly, I almost yelped myself.

I peeked around the corner. Amy sat on the couch facing me, her shoulders shaking as sobs wracked her body. Her head hung and the blonde, messy locks formed a curtain around her face. Poor thing. She seemed absolutely devastated.

"What happened?" Amy finally asked as I hid once again.

"He was murdered."

"Murdered?!" Amy shrieked. "Who in the world would want to kill him?"

"I was hoping you could help me with that," Adam replied. "We can't bring him back, but I would like to get him justice."

The familiar sound of the staircase creaking and moaning met my ears as Cathy descended. "What's going on in here?" she asked. "Why are you screaming, Amy?"

"Colin was murdered!" Amy wailed.

"What!?"

"Oh my word, Cathy," Amy sobbed. "What am I going to do?"

"Duh, duh, duh... The fiancé is finished, Bernie!" Ruby called from the living room, obviously enjoying the new exciting event unfolding.

Amy cried while everyone else remained quiet. After a long stretch of silence, Adam asked, "What's your name, miss?"

"Cathy Willard. I'm a friend of Amy's."

"It's nice to meet you," he said. "Amy, can I ask you a few questions?"

"Y-yes."

"You said Colin was your fiancé. When did you two break up?"

"The day before yesterday," she replied, blowing her nose.

"And what happened to make you call off the wedding?"

"I already told you. He cheated on me."

"*Again*. He cheated on you *again*," Cathy interjected.

"I'm sorry to hear that," Adam said. "Are you from Sedona?"

"No, we live in Phoenix," Amy replied.

"I'm assuming Colin did as well?"

"Yes."

"And what brought you to Sedona?" Adam asked.

"I caught Colin cheating," Amy said. "I'd visited Sedona looking for wedding venues in the spring and loved it up here. Cathy and I actually stayed here at this bed and breakfast. I was so upset, I wanted to get out of town. I remembered how much I'd liked this place, and the next thing I knew, I was driving up here."

"Hey Bernie!" Ruby yelled. "It's too bad you can't see this dramafest. It's a good one!"

Leave it to Ruby to find death amusing. So inappropriate.

"And how did Colin end up here if you two had broken up?"

"He said he was going to win me back," Amy replied. "He came up here wanting to work things out between us."

"So you both arrived yesterday, correct?"

"Yes. I came in the morning and he got here in the afternoon."

"And what about you, Cathy?" Adam asked. "When did you arrive?"

"Amy called me and asked me to come up yesterday," she said. "I couldn't get anyone to cover my shift at work, so I came up this morning."

"When was the last time you spoke to Colin, Amy?" Adam asked.

"Yesterday."

"So you met him, or spoke on the phone?"

"Both."

"What time did you talk to him?"

"I... I don't recall. I can check my phone if you like. But it was the afternoon, early evening."

"Okay, we'll look at your device in a minute. Can you tell me where you were last night?" Adam asked the inevitable question.

"I was here," Amy replied. "The owner can verify that."

Except, I couldn't. I had been with Adam until about ten, and when I'd arrived home, I hadn't seen Amy. He'd ask me about her statement, and poof!—I'd be pulled into yet another murder investigation.

I didn't have to get involved. Just tell him

the truth and allow the wheels of justice to rotate without me.

"I'll ask her about it," Adam said. "What about yesterday afternoon? You were with Colin, correct?"

"For a bit, yes."

"Can you describe what you did, what time, and your interactions with him?"

Amy once again became quiet. "I don't think I like where this discussion is going," she said, the tears now dried up. She barely sounded hoarse or congested. Had she been faking the hysteria from earlier?

"I'm sorry?"

"I think I would prefer to continue this conversation with a lawyer present," she said.

"Is that necessary?" Adam asked. "I'm questioning you about the death of your fiancé. I'm trying to get him justice. Any information you can offer only helps me do that."

"Your tone is accusatory." Amy's voice was clipped. "Like you think I had something to do with him being killed."

"I never mentioned it."

"That's how it feels. I don't want to talk to you anymore. Not without an attorney."

Hmm... interesting. I hadn't heard the so-called accusatory tone Amy had. She'd gone from distraught to snappy pretty quickly.

"I'll be going," Adam said. "And you'll be coming down to the office with me for questioning. We can wait for your attorney there."

"What?!" she shrieked. "I'm not going anywhere!"

"Bernie! Adam's pulling out his handcuffs!" Ruby yelled.

"Yes, you are," he said. "We can do this quietly, or I can put you in handcuffs and you can make a scene. You're under investigation for the murder of Colin Victory. If you aren't going to talk to me here, then we'll do it at the station."

"It's okay, Amy," Cathy said. "Just go. I'll call your parents and tell them what's going on. They'll get you a lawyer."

"I can't believe this!" Amy cried. "My fiancé is murdered and I'm being taken to jail?!"

"You aren't being taken to jail," Adam said. I could tell by the shortness in his voice that he was losing his patience. "You are being taken in, at your request, for questioning with your lawyer."

"You better crawl back to your bedroom," Ruby called from the living room. "Just in case Cathy decides to venture in there after Amy and Adam leave!"

How would I explain sitting on my kitchen floor? I couldn't, except to admit I was eavesdropping. I carefully crawled back to my bedroom door, opened it, and slid through. I shut my eyes as I closed it, hoping I was quiet enough not to arouse suspicion in the living room.

"Boo!" Ruby yelled from behind me.

I bit my lip to keep from screaming and turned around. "I told you not to do that!" I hissed.

"I know, I know. But it's fun. I like getting a rise out of you."

Taking a deep breath, I sank into my rocking chair as Ruby stretched out on my yellow comforter. A second later, Elvira, my tabby, came out from under the bed and curled up next to the ghost.

"What did you make of all that?" I asked.

Ruby shrugged. "I don't know why people always insist on getting attorneys involved. It makes them look guilty."

"I agree, but I understand why they do. No one wants to implicate themselves."

"Mark my words on this one... Amy's guiltier than a sinner at church. She offed Cunning Colin."

"You don't know that based on listening in on that conversation."

"I'm certain," Ruby replied. "I feel it right here in my gut. Besides," she held up three fingers, "the people on those TV murder shows always say there are three reasons to kill someone: love, money and pride. Are we in agreement she loved him?"

"Yes, I suppose so."

"According to Cathy, that turd ruined Amy's pride not once, but multiple times."

"That's true."

"She's got motive. Hell hath no fury like a woman scorned. Or whatever that saying is."

I sighed and stared out the window. No point in arguing with her. Despite Amy's motive, I wasn't convinced she had killed Colin based on what I'd overheard.

But if Ruby was correct, that meant I had a murderer living under my roof.

Yikes.

I didn't like the thought one bit.

CHAPTER 5

The last time I'd been involved in a murder, I'd almost died... twice. First, a man had captured me and threatened to toss me down a four-story stairwell. Second, I was given an overdose of flunitrazepam, a powerful drug for insomniacs as well as a date rape drug when used for nefarious purposes. With those two incidents still haunting me, I'd decided to abide by Ruby's suggestion of taking a self-defense class.

My teacher, Jezebel, owned Tip 'Em Back, the dive bar at the edge of town. Her grandmother, Janis, and Ruby had been besties in life and Jezebel knew my secret—

Ruby's ghost remained stuck on this plane. I'd had to reveal it to her the first time we'd met because Ruby had talked me into trying to cheat at poker in Jezebel's place and we'd been caught. I'd had no other choice than to divulge the truth.

Jezebel gave self-defense classes during the day in the poker room in the back of the bar. As I entered the establishment, I looked forward to taking my mind off the murder. I most certainly wanted to help Darla, but I didn't want to become tangled up in another investigation. Two near-death experiences were enough for me. I'd have to visit her and find out what exactly she wanted me to do to help her through this difficult time.

"You did really great last time, Bernie," Ruby said as she trailed behind me. "I can't wait to watch you kick some butt again!"

I shook my head, knowing she was trying to be encouraging, but she lied. Frankly, I found self-defense difficult at best and had thought about quitting the classes many times. The thought of intentionally striking another person disturbed me.

Jezebel had told me over and over that I wouldn't hurt her, but the hesitation was still there. Perhaps I was simply a yoga-loving pacifist and completely out of my element.

I strode past the wall of old pictures and the large wooden bar to the poker room. The poker table had been moved up against the wall, the chairs stacked in a corner. Jezebel had laid out blue mats on the old wooden floor so when she tossed me around it didn't hurt too badly. "Jezebel?" I called. Perhaps she was in the restroom.

"Wonder where she went?" Ruby muttered.

After waiting a few moments, I yelled for her again and checked the bar area. Nothing.

"You know, it was my idea that they turn this area into a poker room," Ruby said. "Janis used the room as storage, but I saw it as wasted space. Lost revenue. I helped her clean it out and she started the weekly poker game. This room became known as the cash cow, especially when Janis brought in bands to play. On nights the room was empty, I'd set up a table and give psychic readings. I made a lot of money here."

While alive, Ruby had been a semi-famous psychic with her own call-in line. Celebrities often visited her or flew her out to Hollywood.

"You should do that!" She turned to me. "You could give psychic readings here!"

"But I'm not psychic," I replied.

"That's okay. I could teach you how to do it and be here the whole time telling you what to say."

"*Teach* me to give psychic readings?"

"Well, sure. It's not something you just know how to do!"

"Are you telling me you weren't a true psychic either? That you swindled people?"

She stared at me and shook her head. "How absolutely insulting. I may be a lot of things, but a swindler is not one of them. I'm just offering a suggestion to help you bring in more money for my new ATV."

Yes, the ATV. I'd had to sell hers when I moved in and she hadn't let me forget I'd let go of her most prized possession. I had been putting money away to buy us a new one and I was getting close to being able to afford it. I hadn't shared that with Ruby, though. I wanted to surprise her one day.

I shook my head. "I don't have time to give psychic readings. I have enough on my plate. I—"

Thick arms wrapped around my chest and pulled me off balance. I screamed and clawed at the forearms as they tightened around me.

My mind went completely blank as my body stiffened, and I froze. My attacker strengthened their grip and pulled me off my feet. Visions of being slammed against a wall and drugged, completely unable to move, came to mind and panic gripped my chest.

A few seconds later, I was released. I turned to find Jezebel staring at me with irritation. "What the heck am I supposed to do with you? Where's your training?"

"Dear Lord," Ruby muttered, shaking her head and settling in on the mats. "You'd be dead if that had been a real attacker, Bernie."

Placing my hands on my knees, I took some deep breaths. Both were right. I hadn't even put up a little bit of a fight. I'd completely failed.

"Come on," Jezebel said. "Let's warm up." She handed me a jump rope. Since Jezebel had almost made it as a professional MMA fighter, self-defense class wasn't just about self-defense. It was a full body workout that often left me in need of a nap.

"Is Ruby with you today?" she asked.

"Yes," I said, sighing, completely disappointed. I should have been able to at least attempt to defend myself.

"Hey, Ruby!" Jezebel said. "I was thinking about you today and it reminded me to take out the trash."

Ruby cackled for a moment. "Hey, Jezzy! I'll never forget the first time we met. But I'll keep trying."

And they loved to insult each other.

I relayed Ruby's message and Jezebel hooted, pleased with the exchange. The first time Ruby asked me give Jezebel her zinger, I'd been afraid she'd hit me. Instead, she'd had a great comeback and I realized the behavior had been normal for them while Ruby had been alive.

Out of the corner of my eye, I watched Jezebel jump rope. Quick and light on her feet, the muscles in her arms and legs moved with grace. With her full-sleeve tattoo, chiseled body, and the grimace she wore if she didn't know someone, she could come across as very intimidating. Heck, who was I kidding? I'd been coming to see her for just over a month and I still found her somewhat menacing. Perhaps it was because I knew her brawn wasn't all for show. She had the skills to snap me in half.

"So what's new with you? How's business?" she asked, tossing the jump rope to the side. While she had hardly broken a sweat, I could barely breathe. And all this time I had thought I was in pretty good shape. That was until I could see Ruby. My exercise habits had gone south hanging out with her.

"Not a lot," I said. "I'm finally getting a break in the stream of customers, which is good and bad."

"I know what you mean. You need the rest, you want the rest, but the money sure feels nice sitting in your pocket."

"Exactly."

"The same thing happens here at the bar. I'd like to take a week or so off, but I have to keep the doors open. Where would my regulars go? I want them spending their money here, not somewhere else."

"Can you find anyone to cover for you?" I asked.

"Sure, but only for a night or two. No one can manage this place long-term but me."

It was the same problem I'd run into. The last time I'd left the bed and breakfast in someone else's care, there'd been a murder in one of the suites.

"Sorry to break it to you, but there won't be any rest for you today here in class. After your lack of performance, we're starting at the basics again." Jezebel paused for a moment then added, "What should you have done once I had you in the bearhug?"

"Lean forward, which takes you off balance and leaves enough space for me to elbow you."

"Exactly. So why didn't you do that?"

I didn't have an answer. Well, I did, but it

was hard to say. "I... I remembered being attacked at the hotel... being slammed against the wall, being thrown to the concrete steps... stuff like that. I was afraid and I... I couldn't move."

"Sounds like a little PTSD."

"Maybe," I said with a shrug.

"Hey," Jezebel said, placing her hands on my shoulders. "You're learning the skills to never be a victim again. We just need you to recall them when you need them. Let's try the bear hug one more time."

I turned around and she swung her arms around me. Shutting my eyes, I leaned forward, which loosened her grasp enough for me to jam an elbow into her ribs. With a grunt she almost let me go and I turned to face her.

"Perfect!" she yelled. "Now what?"

"Please don't make me hit you," I said, fully knowing what was expected of me: a palm to the nose or a kick to the groin.

Jezebel rolled her eyes. "You aren't going to hurt me, Bernie. Trust me. But if it makes you feel better, we'll just go through the movements so that you develop the memory in case you ever have to use them."

I hoped not. I really, really hoped not. I had no intention of ever putting myself in the middle of a murder investigation again, but that didn't mean I'd never have someone break into my house or some unhinged person on the street attack me. I ran a bed and breakfast and had strangers under my roof a good majority of the time. Being prepared was never a bad thing.

After a few fake palm shots to her nose, she said, "Okay, good. Now let's move on to the hammer strike. Grab your keys."

I hurried to where I'd dumped my purse and retrieved them. The pepper spray hanging from the clasp was new.

"Nice!" Jezebel said, taking the keys from me and fingering the canister. "I love the pepper spray, but here's the issue: you need to unlock it. If you're attacked, are you going to have time to fiddle with it?"

Good point. "Probably not."

"That's right. But you *will* have time to strike your attacker with your keys." She laced them between her knuckles so the metal showed through her gripped fingers like claws. "This will do damage like you can't believe. So don't outright hit me—I'd hate for you to bloody this beautiful face of mine. But practice. Remember what I showed you. The power comes from your core, not your arm."

I took a couple of swings in her general direction.

"That's good, but it comes from here and here," she said, touching my stomach and hips. "Let me get behind you."

As she placed one hand on each of my hips, I swung and she pushed and pulled. "Do you feel the difference?" she asked. "It's not upper body strength. It's core strength."

I lashed out again, and I did notice a change with the modification. "Definitely more powerful," I murmured.

"Exactly. People always think hitting someone is about how strong your arms are. It's not. Hitting someone is all about the torso."

I practiced a few more strikes while Jezebel moved my hips and I imagined an attacker in front of me. My confidence rose with each swing, the strength of the move vibrating through my body.

"Excellent," she said. "You feel good with this one. I can sense it."

"You're right," I said, smiling.

"Tough as nails, Bernie!" Ruby said, standing. "I wouldn't mess with you!"

Jezebel smiled. "Next time, we're going to practice the over-the-shoulder flip and I'll teach you how to break someone's fingers."

I laughed but winced as well. She spoke of violence with such ease, it sometimes made me uncomfortable.

"Come by tonight for a beer," she suggested. "We'll celebrate owning our businesses."

Adam and I were supposed to be heading out to dinner, but I hadn't heard from him. With the murder, I didn't think I would and assumed our dinner plans would be forgotten. Yet, curling up in my bed with a good book sounded much better than bellying up to the bar. "I'll think about it. I've got some things to do tonight."

"You do not," Ruby said. "You're just a homebody."

I smiled and ignored her. "Thanks for the class today, Jezebel. I appreciate it."

"My pleasure! We'll see you Friday for sure! I'll make a knuckle breaker out of you sooner or later!"

I had my doubts but I appreciated her enthusiasm.

Jezebel walked me to the front door and I waved while Ruby and I got into my SUV.

As we pulled out of the parking lot, a police cruiser drove in. Sheriff Walker tipped his cowboy hat at me.

"What's old Bruce doing here?" Ruby asked.

I also wondered, but I continued on my way.

What the sheriff wanted with Jezebel wasn't any of my business.

CHAPTER 6

On my way home, I called Darla, thinking I'd stop by at the diner to say hello and see how she was doing.

"It's not a good time, Bernie," she said, sounding out of breath. "The Sedona Business Association decided to drop in for lunch. I'm swamped right now."

"Is there anything I can do to help?" I was a disaster in the kitchen and she'd certainly politely tell me to stay away, but I asked anyway.

"Are you kidding me? No. I feel like you helping would only make more work for me. But if you can stop by tomorrow, just before noon, we can talk then. I can only concentrate on one thing at a time, and right now I'm trying to figure out why so many in the association like bacon and avocado sandwiches."

"Sounds good. I'll see you tomorrow." I set the phone down in my drink holder. My feelings should probably have been hurt, but I actually sighed with relief. Cooking wasn't my specialty.

"Normally I'd say I don't want to go see Darla, but tomorrow's a different story," Ruby said.

"Why is that?"

"I don't know. Ever since her diagnosis, I've been feeling bad for her. I want to go with you. I know she won't know I'm there, but I want to see her."

Ruby had never liked Darla, always saying she found her boring. But since we found out Darla suffers from schizophrenia, Ruby had softened her stance a bit. "That's fine," I replied. "Happy to have you tag along."

At some point, I felt it was only right

that I tell Darla about Ruby, but now wasn't the time. She had enough on her plate, her mental health rightfully being her top priority. Making her aware of my unruly ghost could possibly only make her condition worse. I didn't want to be responsible for that.

With a sigh, I pulled into the dirt parking lot behind my house. My shoulders had begun to ache from my workout with Jezebel. Tomorrow I would be very sore so I made a mental note to grab some ibuprofen once I got inside.

I unlocked the back door and headed into the kitchen. For some reason, I was surprised to find Cathy sitting on a stool at the counter with a bottle of wine in front of her, a glass in her hand.

Frankly, I'd completely forgotten I still had guests around. "Hey," I said. "How are things going?"

"Terrible," she muttered as she sipped her glass. "Hope you don't mind me breaking into your wine stash."

I glanced into the living room at the

wine display set up on the side table—a few bottles of red and a couple white along with a half-dozen glasses. "No worries. That's why it's there."

"I figured."

"Do you mind if I join you?"

"Not at all. I'd appreciate the company."

I grabbed a glass for myself and sat down on the stool next to her. She poured me a large portion of chardonnay.

"This is really tasty wine," she said.

"It's from an Arizona winery located in Cottonwood," I said. "They have tours and tastings. It's not too far from here. Maybe you and Amy should go once this whole mess with Colin is straightened out. It makes for a fun girls' day." I had gone once with Darla about a year prior, and we'd had a really good time. "Have you heard from Amy at all? What's going on with the investigation?"

Despite my promise to myself to not get involved in the homicide, I wasn't above fishing for information.

"She throws the line and begins to reel it

in!" Ruby said from behind me. "Will she get a bite?"

"I don't know what's going on with the investigation," Cathy said, shaking her head. "I can't believe the sheriff brought Amy into the station like that."

"And you called her parents?"

Cathy nodded. "I've grown really close to them since Amy and I lived in college. They have friends who live up here, so I thought maybe they'd know of a good attorney. Turns out I was right."

"Did they give you a name?"

"Yes. Richard Drinkwater."

"Oh, he's good," Ruby said. "He represented me in my streaking on the golf course case."

I fought a snort.

I'd never heard of him, but I'd never needed an attorney, either. "Why do you think she clammed up?" I took a long sip of wine as I eyed my guest over the glass, surprised Cathy was being so open.

"She did the right thing. If you didn't notice, when Amy's in a good mood, she's quite chatty. I think she's afraid she's going to say something she'll regret or that will put the blame on her."

We sat in silence for a long moment as we sipped our wine. "Can you tell me about Colin?" I asked.

Cathy shook her head and sighed heavily. "I actually dated him in high school. It didn't last long because he was sleeping with anyone who would give him a second glance. We were young and that guy broke my heart."

Interesting. "Really? When did you and Amy meet?"

"In college, at ASU. We both lived in the dorms and became fast friends and moved into an off-campus apartment together. Our junior year of college she started dating him. Imagine my surprise when she introduced us."

"I bet. How did you feel about that?"

"It had been so long since I'd even laid eyes on Colin, it didn't matter to me. I warned Amy about him, but she told me people changed. He wasn't the same guy he was in high school, and she had a point. I knew I was different, so I assumed he was as well."

"How long did they date before he proposed?" I asked.

"On and off for a total of about three years."

"That's quite a long time."

"Yes."

"How many times did he cheat?"

"Twice that I'm aware of. I have a feeling it was more, but Amy hid it from me."

"And she stuck around?"

"They'd break up and then he'd beg her to come back. Send flowers, bring her jewelry, and promise he'd never do it again. She actually quit seeing him for a bit right before we graduated from college. Then his parents were killed and he called her."

"Oh, wow. When was that?"

"Maybe two years ago? About six months before he proposed. Colin was devastated over their deaths."

"What happened?" I asked, imagining it was something besides illness to have taken them both at the same time.

"His parents were at a party and his father had too much to drink. He caused a three-car pileup on the freeway and killed not only himself and his wife, but two other people as well."

I winced at the tragedy. "How horrible," I murmured. "Does Colin have any other family?"

Cathy shrugged. "He had an older sister when we dated in high school. If I remember right, her name was Jessica. It's my understanding that after she graduated, she simply disappeared. No one in Colin's family really knew what happened to her. Amy told me Colin thought it was probably drugs because Jessica would show up every now and then looking pretty rough and asking for money."

"Any other siblings?"

"Not that I'm aware of. When I dated Colin, I think I met his parents twice and his sister once. We were young and didn't talk much about our families. Instead, we were too busy trying to be cool." Cathy shook her head and laughed. "Boy, did I fail at being cool."

So had I, but reminiscing on my awk-

ward teenage years wouldn't get me information on the murder that I wasn't going to
become involved in. "But Amy hasn't mentioned any other brothers or sisters?"

"Nope." Cathy reached for the wine
bottle and poured another glass. "I hope she
comes back soon. She can get a little defiant
when she's upset. I hope she doesn't say
anything that gets her in trouble."

We sat in silence for a long stretch of
time, my thoughts wandering as Ruby
hummed *Beast of Burden* from the Rolling
Stones. I knew so little about Amy, Cathy,
and even less about Colin. But curiosity got
the best of me, so I continued to prod.

"What did Colin do for a living?"

"He was an attorney," she replied. "He'd
graduated law school not too long ago and
landed a job at the firm where his dad had
been partner."

"And Amy?"

"She's in pharmaceutical sales, but in between jobs right now."

"What about you?" I remembered Cathy
said she couldn't get anyone to cover her
shift when Amy had summoned her up to

Sedona, so she'd had to leave early in the morning.

"My sociology degree has done wonders for me," Cathy replied. "I currently work in a warehouse."

"Nothing wrong with that," I said.

"Let's just say I had loftier goals."

The front door chimes rang and both of us turned. Amy marched in and threw her purse onto the couch.

"Hey!" Cathy hurried over to her friend. "What happened? Are you okay?"

Amy shook her head and began to sob. "I'm so upset right now, I'm not sure whether to cry or scream."

"Well, you're crying right now, so scream if you want." She took Amy into an embrace.

"Oh, for everything holy, no screaming," Ruby said, sidling up next to me. "This should be good. Can't wait to hear what she has to say about her visit down to the sheriff's station."

"You and me both," I muttered softly.

"Come in and have a glass of wine," Cathy said. "Tell us everything."

"I really need a shower," Amy replied. "I feel so dirty after being in the police station like I'm some criminal."

"Well, if you murdered Cunning Colin, you are, honey," Ruby pointed out.

Amy hurried up the stairs and Cathy turned to me. "Last time we were here, we never took you up on the sunset yoga. Do you still offer that?"

I nodded and smiled. Sunset yoga took place on the upper deck facing east. It had been a while since a customer had requested the service, but I found myself looking forward to it. "I'll go get dressed."

"Amy loves yoga, and I think it would do her some good right now," Cathy said. "I'll tell her we'll be joining you."

"You need to get Amy alone and find out what she told the sheriff," Ruby said, trailing behind me as I strode through the kitchen.

I didn't reply until we were safely behind the closed bedroom door. "Why is that?"

Ruby sighed as she lay across the mattress. "I don't know, Bernie. There's something about Cathy I don't trust."

I slipped off my jeans and pulled on a

pair of leggings. "Well, you have to have a reason not to trust someone."

"No, I don't. The girl strikes me as someone who would sell out her own mother."

"I have no idea how you're catching that vibe," I mustered. "Yes, in the past she's been eerily quiet, but she seems fine now. Maybe she and Amy just have one of those friendships where one of them always does the talking for the both of them."

"Never heard of such a thing."

"That's because I guarantee if you've ever had a relationship like that, you were the one doing the talking."

Ruby snorted and chuckled. "That may be true, but there's something off about that woman. Trust me."

"Are you saying that you think she killed Colin?"

"Probably not," Ruby replied. "I'm not sure what her motive would be. Being cheated on in high school is a silly grudge to hold, but maybe she has."

"That was a decade ago. I find it hard to

believe that she'd wait ten years to exact her revenge on her broken teenage heart."

"You're right," Ruby said. "It does sound far-fetched, but I still don't trust her."

"But you can't tell me why."

"That's right. I have no idea why, but that girl is bad news."

CHAPTER 7

With Ruby in tow, I arrived at Darla's right at eleven the next day as she'd requested. When I walked into the diner, I was surprised to find so few customers. Darling's Diner used to be a thriving place, oftentimes with a wait for a table. I counted five people eating.

Darla had done the decorating. Pictures of the greater Sedona area she'd taken herself—the cliffs, the desert, the wildlife—covered the taupe walls. I'd been with her when some of them had been snapped, and they brought back fond memories of our friendship.

"Hey," she said, coming out from the

kitchen wiping her hands on a towel. "Sally just arrived, so I've got an hour break. Do you want to go upstairs?"

I nodded and followed her through the kitchen. When we reached the bottom of the staircase leading up to her apartment, she removed her apron and carefully hung it on a hook. The old wooden stairs creaked under our weight as we climbed. My arms ached as I grabbed the railing and I debated whether I should cancel my self-defense classes for the rest of the week.

Darla sighed as we entered the apartment. I inhaled the scent of bacon and roses. Multi-colored pillows covered the white sofa, a blue blanket had been tossed over the back. The galley kitchen sparkled under the stream of sunlight flooding through the windows. I did like the space my big house offered, but Darla's apartment always made me want to settle into the couch and take a long nap. Cozy was the perfect description.

"Do you want some coffee?" Darla asked.

I sat on the couch. "Sounds great. Thank you."

A few moments later, she brought over two pink mugs covered in red and white hearts that read, *Be a darling! Eat at Darling's Diner!*

I tasted cinnamon, nutmeg, and vanilla. "Wow, Darla. This is delicious."

"Thanks. It's a little spice concoction I made up."

"You should package it up and sell it," I said, taking another sip.

"Do you think it's that good?"

"Definitely."

"I wish I could catch a whiff," Ruby said wistfully. She'd been so quiet, I had almost forgotten she'd come with me.

Darla tucked a lock of blonde hair behind her ear and seemed much calmer than she had when she'd visited my house the other day.

"So yesterday was busy?" I asked, recalling the Sedona Business Association had dropped in.

"Thankfully, yes. My business has tanked since I had to close the doors and take care of my mental health."

"Why do you think that is?"

"There are all sorts of rumors as to why. Most of them mentioning that I'd been closed by regulators for uncleanliness, which we both know wasn't true."

I nodded, but in a way, she was wrong. When Darla quit taking her medication, her restaurant had suffered. Our friend Jack had made the call to shut it down for that exact reason. Her mother had agreed running the diner had been too much for her at that point, and the restaurant remained closed until she could get back on her feet. So yes, it had been shuttered due to the roach scurrying across the floor, but Darla's schizophrenia had been the core reason.

"I'm really struggling, Bernie, and I need some help."

"What can I do?"

"I need you to find out who killed that guy at the hotel... I can't remember his name."

"Colin?"

"Yes. How do you know that?"

"I'm dating a deputy," I said, even though Adam and I hadn't discussed the case at all. It seemed better to use him as an excuse instead of informing her I may have a killer staying with me. For some reason, I felt it best to keep that news to myself.

"Looks like Starsky and Hutch are back at it again," Ruby yelled with a whoop. "We're on the case!"

"That's a job for the police," I said gently. "Not me."

"But you've solved two other murders," Darla said. "I didn't kill that man, but the sheriff is pointing his fingers in my direction."

"They interviewed you, right? Have they been back?"

Darla nodded. "The sheriff told me that they'd be making an arrest soon and I shouldn't leave town." She wiped a tear tracking down her cheek. "If you find the murderer, then I don't have that weight hanging over me. Right now, it feels like an anvil about to drop. And I hear people whispering about me. One customer even said that because I have a mental illness, surely I'm the one who killed him. Like everyone who does have a mental illness is some type of psychopath and capable of murder."

I knew for a fact that some people with schizophrenia were capable of killing others, but I didn't believe Darla was. At least, I hoped not.

"The police will find out who killed him and arrest them," I said, trying to soothe my friend. "We know you didn't."

"That's what I'm telling you, Bernie!" she yelled. "Please stop trying to placate me and telling me everything's okay! It's not. They're going to throw me in jail for a crime I didn't commit!"

The outburst caught me by surprise and I almost spilled my coffee. I set down my cup. "Okay, okay," I said, holding up my hands in front of me. "Tell me again what happened that night."

Darla took a couple of deep breaths and shut her eyes for a moment. When she focused on me, she seemed much calmer.

"I had the sign out indicating I was closed. He came in and said he wanted a milkshake and a sandwich."

"Right. You said before he was belligerent, that he swore a lot."

"Yes. I think he was drunk."

"Really?"

"Yes. When I think about my conversation with him, it seemed like he slurred his words a bit."

"Okay, what else did the police say?"

"They were really interested in my knives. I have a set missing one, and they took it, saying the brand is the same as the one they found in his chest. It's also identical to the set I bought you for Christmas last year."

The news stunned me. The murder weapon was the same make as a knife set in Darla's kitchen? I stared at her a long moment, my heart thundering. Was I sitting next to a murderer?

"Sheriff Walker said they were going to match it up and do some DNA sampling on it, and then he'd be coming for me," Darla continued. "I'm scared, Bernie. My mental health is too fragile for this additional stress. I feel like I'm going to lose my mind."

I took her hand in mine and squeezed her fingers. "Are you taking your medication?"

She nodded.

"Don't stop, okay?"

"I won't."

"Now what else did they say? Did they give you any indication on what this guy was up to before he showed up at your place?"

"No. But they have a really tight theory of me being the killer."

I made a mental note to ask Adam what Colin had been up to before arriving at Darla's. Would it matter? I wasn't sure, but it might. "What's their theory?"

"That night when he stiffed me and I called the police, I told them every detail of my run-in with him. Part of that was him telling me where he was staying in case I wanted to try to collect from him. According to the sheriff, after Colin left I was so angry I called the police. After I was finished with them, I grabbed a knife and went to the Sedona Grand Hotel, found out which room he was in, then somehow got him to open the door for me and stabbed him."

"That's a lot of anger to be carrying

around," Ruby said. I started at her voice. Why was she being so quiet?

Darla took another sip of her coffee. "I don't have an alibi. Like I told you, I came up here and watched television, then went to bed. I didn't speak to anyone and no one saw me that night."

She definitely found herself in a bit of a pickle. With Colin stiffing her on the bill, her knife matching the murder weapon and no one to vouch for her whereabouts, the police had a good case against her.

"I don't have the energy to pull anything like that," Darla continued. "I'm running on fumes, Bernie. With this extra pressure, I feel like I'm going to burn out. Taking care of myself is slowly falling on my priorities list. Instead, I'm worrying, which means I'm not sleeping."

"And you want me to find the true killer to clear you?"

"Yes. You've already solved two cases and you're dating Adam. You can help to steer the whole department in the right direction."

The last thing I wanted was to be involved in another murder investigation. The idea ramped up my own anxiety, flashbacks of being chased and drugged playing before my eyes. However, I hated seeing my friend so upset and obviously suffering. "I'll see what I can find out," I said in a noncommittal tone. "I'll talk to Adam. At least I can let you know what direction the investigation is taking. Maybe if you have an idea of their evidence against you compared to what they have on the other suspects, you'll be able to put your mind at ease."

"Does that mean we get to go visit Nutjob Ned?" Ruby asked.

"Thanks a lot, Bernie," Darla said as we both stood and she embraced me. "I knew I could count on you. Yes, I would feel a lot better just knowing that they're looking at other people besides me. Thank you."

"They are," I promised. "I'll be in touch."

Ruby remained quiet as we hurried down the stairs, through the diner and out to the car. I saw Jack over at Jumping Jack Jeep Tours and waved, hoping he wouldn't mosey on over to say hello. Thankfully, he stayed put, but motioned me to call him. I gave him the thumbs up.

"Oh, look!" Ruby said. "Mr. Dimples! My goodness, he gets cuter every time I lay eyes on him, even with all that machine oil on him. Makes him look rugged and sexy. Like he wasn't sexy enough, but you know what I mean."

Jack serviced all the ATVs he rented out and Jeeps for the tours he conducted, so one could often find him covered in automobile fluids.

"What do you think?" Ruby asked once we were in the car.

"About what?"

"Do you think Darla offed Colin?"

I shook my head. "No. What about you?"

"Wow, Bernie. I'm not sure about that one. The police have a pretty good case against her, especially with that knife missing. But it can't hurt to casually question Adam about it and see if the sheriff is feeding Darla a line of bull or if he's really got her in his sights."

"I think he's full of it. He's trying to scare her."

"Perhaps you're right," Ruby said, sighing. "But if talking to Adam makes Darla feel better, it can't hurt."

I backed out of the parking spot and headed to the street. "I have to admit, I'm surprised by your sympathy toward her."

"Yeah, me too. Let's go see Adam so we can put Darla's mind at ease."

We drove for a few moments and I glanced over at my ghost. "You've been pretty quiet recently."

"So?"

"It's not like you."

Ruby shrugged and turned her head to the passenger window. "I've just had a lot on my mind."

"Like what?"

"Never mind, Bernie. We've got another murder to solve, so let's get to it! To Adam's!"

"I'll call first and make sure it's okay. He may not even be home."

"You shouldn't operate a car while talking on the phone," Ruby chided.

"And you shouldn't take your clothes off and run down a fairway at a golf course."

Ruby laughed as I dialed. "Touché, Bernie. Touché."

When Adam didn't answer, I set down my phone. "I don't want to be involved in another murder, Ruby," I said softly. "The thought terrifies me."

"You don't have anything to worry about. You're doing great with your self-defense classes and I'm here for you."

I sighed but didn't reply.

Like Ruby being there for me had done any good last time.

I wouldn't put myself in danger again, but I would do my best to help my friend.

CHAPTER 8

*W*hen we arrived home, I found Amy sitting on one of the living room couches reading an old -fashioned paperback book—no e-reader for her. A girl after my own heart.

"How's the book?" I asked.

"Really good. I figured a mystery would take my mind off Colin."

"Is it working?"

She shook her head and set down the book on the cushion next to her. The sun streamed in through the windows causing her blonde locks to gleam golden. "I can't stop thinking about him and wondering who killed him."

I sat down across from her, hoping I wasn't overstepping my bounds, but I needed information. It appeared to be the perfect time to fish for it. "What happened that night, Amy?"

"Very direct," Ruby said. "I like it. No small talk or beating around the bush with this one."

I didn't want to ask if it was okay to discuss the murder. I just wanted answers. The fastest way seemed to be pointed questions.

"Do you have any coffee?" Amy asked. "I'm not sleeping well and I shouldn't have any this late in the afternoon, but I'd love a cup."

"Of course," I said, standing. "Let me make a fresh pot and we can talk."

"I'd appreciate it. Thank you."

As I hurried into the kitchen, Ruby trailed behind me.

"She's asking for coffee so she can gather her thoughts and make sure her story doesn't vary from the one she told the police."

I hadn't considered that line of thinking but perhaps Ruby was right. Would Amy even think I'd go to the police? I tried to remember if she was aware Adam and I dated, and I didn't see any way she could know unless something happened when she visited in the spring. There shouldn't be a reason for her to be skeptical of sharing what had happened between her and Colin with me.

"You're going to get a lot of information out of this one," Ruby said. "She's ready to spill her guts and confess."

"We don't know that," I whispered as I filled the pot with water and poured it into the coffee maker.

"I'm telling you, she's guilty."

As the coffee dripped into the pot, I pulled out a small, red plastic tray to carry the cream, sugar and two mugs. I'd debated getting a sterling silver serving tray, but it seemed so old-fashioned. I also liked how I didn't have to worry about spilling on the red one—something that happened often. And it went into the dishwasher, which I loved. If I actually bought a silver tray, I'd most likely keep it hidden in the cupboard out of sheer laziness.

Once the coffee had brewed, I poured it into the cups and carried the tray out to the living room.

"Here you go," I said, setting it down on the table between us. "If it's okay, I'm going to join you. I could definitely use a pick-me-up."

"Please do." Amy poured cream and sugar into one of the cups. "I guess I don't have to worry about fitting into a wedding dress any longer," she muttered, then dumped a second spoonful of sugar into her mug.

"Where's Cathy?" I asked, settling back against the cushions.

"She had errands to run. I'm not sure what she's doing. I'm so glad she came up when I asked her to though. She's been my rock through my whole adult life. With Colin's death, I think I would have lost my mind without her."

"It's nice to have a friend like that," I said, thinking of Darla. I'd somehow stepped into the role of being her rock during this whole mess, and I wanted to be there for her and soothe her concerns. I had to discover everything I could about the investigation. "Amy, what happened the night Colin died?"

She sighed and shook her head. "I've been wondering that myself. Who could have killed him?"

"We all want to know, sweetheart," Ruby said. "Just confess your guilt right now."

Amy blew on her cup and took a sip. "I went to see Colin at the Sedona Grand Hotel. I agreed to meet him in his room. I was hesitant at first because he's so sweet when he wants to be and I thought I would have a better chance of standing my ground if we met in public. There wouldn't be a scene. But he convinced me to go to his room so we could have a deep heart-to-heart talk without interruption or distraction."

"He wanted to smooth talk her in private," Ruby said in disgust. "The more I hear about Colin, the less I like him."

"When I arrived, he met me at the door with a dozen roses and a bottle of champagne," Amy continued. "Which was weird since I'd already told him the wedding was off."

"Seems more like a celebration than

someone saying he's sorry for being a no-good, cheating, lying scumbag," Ruby said.

I had to agree.

"Like we had something to celebrate!" Amy continued. "I couldn't believe him! When I walked in, he tried to kiss me, but I told him no. So he became desperate, begging me for forgiveness. Tears and everything. He said he couldn't live without me."

"What did you tell him?" I asked.

"That I deserved respect, and respect meant he didn't run around cheating on me. People in love don't do things like that. Anyway, we fought. There was a lot of yelling. A lot of tears. But I stood my ground and told him our relationship was over. He was very angry with me, but not nearly as mad as I was at him. I'd planned the wedding! I have my dress and the venue booked. The invitations had been sent out. I'd sat through cake tastings and picked a caterer. I was ready to be married, but I couldn't marry someone I couldn't trust."

"That's understandable," I replied, sipping more coffee and regretting it. I could already feel the caffeine coursing through me. It would be a long night before sleep visited me.

"It wasn't the first time Colin had cheated. Did you know I walked in on him with someone *in our bed?* In our apartment?"

"I wasn't aware of that," I said softly. "I'm sorry."

"Caught buck naked and red handed," Ruby said. "You don't get any guiltier than that."

"He was such a jerk." Amy shook her head. "I called the wedding venue today and they aren't returning my deposit. I've not only lost the person I loved, but so much money."

"Money's always a good motive for murder," Ruby mused. "Maybe she thought if she killed him, the venue would have pity on her and return the deposit."

"At least the caterer is being kind and giving me my money back," Amy said. "The wedding was supposed to be in two weeks."

"I'm sorry, Amy."

She began to cry and excused herself to the bathroom.

"A total faker," Ruby said. "Oscar-worthy performance."

"I think she's genuinely upset," I whispered. "You sure want her to be the killer. Have you given any thought to what that means? A murderer under our roof?"

Ruby shrugged and laid her hand over my forearm. "Wouldn't be the first time." A chill traveled down my spine at her ghostly touch.

A few minutes passed and when Amy returned, she'd regained her composure.

"What happened after you left Colin at the hotel?" I asked. "Did you come back to the bed and breakfast?"

Amy shook her head. "No. I walked around for a little while, then I came back here. The next thing I knew, I was being dragged down to the station, accused of murdering the man I was going to marry."

"That must have been quite jarring."

"You have no idea. I felt like I'd entered an alternate universe."

"What happened at the station?"

"Well, the deputy who came here to interview me was nice, but his boss... his boss is a jerk."

Adam. My heart swelled with pride knowing he had continued to be professional with Amy after he'd taken her in. I had no reason to think he'd be anything else, but it still made me incredibly happy.

"Sounds like old Bruce," Ruby muttered. "A jerk to his core."

"What happened when you got to the station?"

"Well, they put me into an interrogation room where I basically sat for a few hours while waiting for a lawyer. I was terrified. I couldn't get out and they left me alone for such long periods of time, I thought they'd forgotten about me. When my lawyer finally came, they brought him in to see me. The sheriff joined us and the three of us sat down and he began questioning me."

"What type of questions was he asking you?"

"How long I'd been with Colin, what our relationship had been like, why I'd left him... things like that. The way the sheriff looked at me was so intimidating—like he already knew what I was thinking before I said anything."

"Tell her not to worry, though," Ruby said. "He's more bark than bite."

I decided to forego the advice for Amy. She didn't need my ghost's input.

"Then he asked where I was that night and who I was with," Amy continued, staring into her coffee cup. "I explained I'd met Colin to discuss our relationship and when I'd left him at the hotel, I had told him it was over between us. Then I went for a walk and came back here." She turned her gaze to me, her brow furrowed as if she couldn't quite remember something. "We saw each other that night, didn't we?"

Pursing my lips together, I shook my head. "I don't think so. I was out late and I don't recall seeing you when I got home."

"You're probably right," Amy said closing her eyes and placing her forehead in her palm. "I was so upset, I dreamt it or something. I told them I saw you, so there's another piece of evidence against me, unless you tell them you and I *did* talk that night."

I smiled but didn't answer. I didn't have

the heart to tell her I would have to rectify the statement she gave the police if they asked me about it. I wasn't getting involved in the investigation, and I wasn't going to lie for her, either.

"What else did they say?" I asked.

"They were going to make an arrest pretty soon," Amy said, sighing. "They have a ton of evidence and it's pretty much an open and shut case."

I rolled my eyes because I'd heard that one before. It was the same thing they'd told Darla. And in the last murder investigation —where a tourist had gone over a cliff— they'd also said the exact same thing. I took it to mean the police had no idea of who they were going to arrest, just like they hadn't before.

"What evidence?" I asked. "Did they show you what that is?"

Amy shrugged. "I don't know. That's what they said: they were going to make an arrest and then they told me not to leave town."

"I'm sorry, Amy," I said, truly saddened by her plight, but my alarm bells were also going off. Why would she tell the cops she'd spoken to me that night? Had she been confused, as she'd indicated, or did she need an alibi and hoped I would provide one?

"Did they say anything else?" I asked.

"Not really, just that I had the motive and the means to kill my fiancé. Apparently, I'm the jilted girlfriend. He'd cheated on me one too many times and I stuck a knife in his heart."

"A perfect crime of passion," Ruby said. "She's absolutely guilty."

CHAPTER 9

*A*dam and I had been playing phone tag. When we finally connected, he asked me to meet him at his condo the next morning. With the way Ruby was jumping up and down, one would think I'd just bought her a new ATV, which made me consider that she was indeed sweet on Ned. The two made for a strange pair. With both being from different centuries, I would think they wouldn't have much in common. But they seemed to get along and my guess was because they had both been trouble-causers while alive. Apparently, some traits bound people through decades.

I stopped at Canyon Coffee and picked

up two lattes and two blueberry scones. How far I'd come—or how far I'd fallen—I wasn't quite sure which applied to me. Six months ago, you wouldn't have caught me dead with such sweet treats, and now my mouth watered just carrying them around. Ruby had played a huge part in my relaxing my eating and exercise habits, and my tight jeans showed it.

When we arrived, Ruby quickly ghosted through the door and I heard her and Ned talking before Adam answered.

"There she is," Adam said as he opened the panel. "I'm so glad to see you."

"It feels like I haven't seen you in weeks!" I gushed, wrapping my arms around his waist.

"It does, but it's only been a couple of days. Come on in and tell me what you've been up to."

I followed him into the tidy living room and took a seat on the couch. After handing him a scone, I bit into mine and groaned. "Delicious."

As we ate, I told him about my self-defense class and how I froze up when Jezebel attacked me. I was able to laugh about it a bit now. "When it happened, I was completely immobile. It was the strangest thing... like I'd become paralyzed."

"It'll become a natural response and not something you need to think about," Adam said. "We have to go through hand-to-hand training like that as well. It's hard at first, but it does become easier."

"That's good to know," I replied. "I want to have it become second nature to me. Maybe you and I can practice together sometime."

"That could be fun," Adam said with a wink. "I wouldn't mind rolling around the floor with you."

A deep blush crawled up my cheeks. Frankly, I wouldn't mind it either.

I also brought up my visit with Darla. Although I attempted to keep the conversation light, my discussion with her weighed heavily on me, especially with how much she was struggling with being named a suspect. "She's certain you're gunning for her."

Adam shrugged. "She's definitely on our radar."

My stomach clenched as I set down my coffee cup. "Seriously, Adam?"

He nodded. "Absolutely. We have a ton of evidence against her."

"What's her motive?"

"For starters, the fact that Colin was a complete jerk to her. He stiffed her and then she's got a mental illness."

Bile rose in my throat as I squeezed my nails into my palms. "So you think she's guilty because of her mental illness?"

"It's a possibility and something we take very seriously. A lot of people with mental illness commit crimes."

Heat warmed my cheeks as my anger slowly rose. "Adam, she didn't kill a complete stranger because he was rude to her and she has a mental illness."

"Like I said, there's a lot of evidence against her. But let's talk about something else. Is Ruby here with you?"

I glanced over at the ghosts, both staring at us. Furious with Adam, I didn't want to discuss anything else. I had to protect my friend. "Yes, she's here. Both she and Ned are looking at us."

"Miss Bernadette seems a little upset," Ned said, crossing his arms over his bloodied chest.

"Oh, you're right on that one," Ruby muttered. "Her knickers are in a big old knot."

"How does that happen?" Ned asked. "Her knickers knotting? That must be terribly uncomfortable."

"It's just a phrase, silly." Ruby chuckled and rolled her eyes. "It means she's upset."

"What have you two been up to?" Adam asked, seemingly unaware of how angry I was.

"Not a lot," I replied. *Just trying to keep Darla calm so she doesn't have some sort of breakdown.*

"Look, Bernie. I can tell you're upset, but I can't talk about the case with you."

"Yes, you can," I said. "I'm not going to say anything to anyone. Just tell me if Darla is really the only suspect you're looking at."

"No. There are three others."

Three others? That sounded promising. "Who?"

"Well, Amy, of course."

"I figured that. You realize she's got more motive than Darla. Colin cheated on her multiple times. It could have been a crime of passion."

"Yes, it's possible."

"That's who my bet is on," Ruby said to Ned. "The jilted girlfriend."

Ned nodded. "Sounds correct. A scorned woman is no one to mess with."

Ruby smiled. "You're a smart one, Ned. We're going to be fantastic friends."

At least the ghosts weren't yelling or fighting with each other any longer. "Who's the third suspect?" I asked.

Adam sighed and shook his head. "Bernie..."

"I'm not asking to be involved or even for particulars of the case!" I threw up my hands. "I'm curious!"

"Fine. As long as you promise me that you aren't going to attempt to solve this investigation yourself."

"I promise," I said. "I'm not putting myself in that position again."

"It might be a good idea to cross your fingers behind your back," Ruby interjected.

"In case you do decide to stick your nose where it doesn't belong in the near future."

She was wrong. I had every intention of staying out of the investigation. Finger crosses weren't necessary. I just wanted to protect Darla. To do that, I had to talk through the case with Adam and make him realize she was innocent.

Adam took another sip of his coffee. "Here's the thing: in a short period of time, Colin angered quite a few people. We've been able to trace his movements through town, and he was a busy boy."

"What happened?" I asked.

"First, he met with Amy in the hotel room where according to her, they fought."

"And Amy went back to my place."

"Speaking of which, did you speak with her that night after you arrived at home?"

"No. I was with you, and then I went straight to bed. I'm not certain she was there."

"She told me that you two did in fact see each other and you talked."

I shook my head and took another sip of coffee. I wouldn't lie to the police and if my truthful information helped clear Darla, all the better. A bit of guilt tugged at me for throwing Amy under the bus, but I had to stick to the facts.

"After his discussion with Amy, he then when down to the hotel bar where he got drunk and almost came to blows with another customer, Mr. Grady. The hotel staff kicked Colin out and told him to go to bed."

"I'm guessing he didn't?"

"Right. He found his way to Tip 'Em Back." Adam took a bite of the scone and then a long sip of coffee. "This is so tasty. Thanks for bringing it."

"How did you know Colin went to Tip 'Em Back?" I asked.

"Because Jezebel called in a disturbance at her place and identified Colin from the name on his credit card."

"Oh, wow. What did he do there?"

"First, he hit on Jezebel, and she made it clear that she wouldn't put up with any of his shenanigans. Then, he actually grabbed another female customer. At that point, Jezebel kicked him out."

"Is Jezebel a suspect?" I asked, a sinking feeling settling in my stomach.

"Yes. She had a few choice words to say to the officer who took her statement that night."

"Like what?"

"She mentioned that if he ever stepped foot into her establishment again, she'd do more than beat him up. She'd kill him. Needless to say, she was pretty upset with his behavior."

I ran my hand through my hair as panic constricted my chest. "She beat him up?"

"Apparently. We thought the bruises on his face were from the skirmish he'd had with the person who murdered him, but Jezebel admitted to hitting him."

"That doesn't mean she killed him."

"No, but it's a possibility we need to examine."

"But she said she'd kill him if he stepped foot in her place again, not kill him just because she was angry."

Adam shrugged. "Maybe she decided to go through with it before he came back."

I smiled and tried to remain calm. Now I

had not only Darla, but Jezebel on the police radar for the same murder. I didn't think either of them killed anyone, but if I had to choose between the two, I'd say Jezebel had more gumption to pull off a murder than Darla.

"Take some deep breaths," Ruby said. "You look like you're about to pass out." I did as instructed. "If he thinks for a second I'm letting Jezzy go down for this, he's quite mistaken."

"Who's Jezzy?" Ned asked.

Ruby lowered her voice as she spoke, making it impossible for me to hear.

"Are you okay?" Adam asked.

"Yes. I just can't believe that Jezebel's a suspect as well."

"We have to investigate everyone, Bernie. You know that."

It was true, but I didn't have to like it. "Did he go anywhere else after Tip 'Em Back, or did he make his way to Darla's for a late-night sandwich?"

"As far as we can tell, he went to Darla's."

"Where he was a rude jerk and stiffed her."

"Yes."

"But he could've gone somewhere else and angered another person who might have killed him."

"He could have, Bernie. No one is discounting you or disagreeing with you."

I nodded, trying to keep the peace between Adam and me, but my anxiety only made me want to push Darla's innocence further.

"Why wasn't he arrested when Jezebel called the cops on him?"

"He was long gone," Adam said. "Same for when Darla phoned it in. Two different deputies took the reports. It wasn't until the next day that we realized the victim, the guy at Darla's and the man harassing women at Tip 'Em Back, were one and the same."

If only they'd been able to arrest him at Jezebel's. Darla would have never been involved and the investigation would be something I would read about in the paper.

"We have some other interesting evidence that we're waiting on," Adam said. "Hopefully, it will nail the murderer without any lingering doubts."

"What's that?"

"Well, we're doing forensics to match up Darla's knife set to the knife that killed Colin. We're also waiting on the hotel to provide us with security footage of the hotel corridor that night. If we can get a clear enough picture, we'll know who the murderer is."

Relief swept through me, calming the heaviness in my chest. "That will certainly prove Darla's innocence, as well as Jezebel's. It's probably that guy Colin fought with in the bar."

"We'll see." He glanced over in the general direction of the ghosts. "What are the two poltergeists up to?"

"I'm not sure," I murmured, watching them as they continued to speak in low tones. "My guess is nothing but trouble."

"We want to go play with the cars again," Ruby said. "We had so much fun before!"

"Yes," Ned agreed.

I turned to Adam. "They want to play in traffic."

He burst out laughing and shook his head. "Can't do it. I've got to get to the office. Sorry, guys. But if you want to go without me, have at it."

"I actually have to go," I said. "I've got a busy day as well."

"Doing what?" Ruby asked. "Let's go have a little bit of fun!"

Ignoring her complaints, I gave Adam a quick kiss. "Have a great day."

"I'll call you later, okay?"

"Sounds good."

As we strode to the car, Ruby asked, "What are we doing now?" Her voice dripped with disappointment.

"Going to see Jezebel."

She perked up immediately. "Oh! That's even more fun than playing chicken in traffic! What a fantastic idea, Bernie!"

I wanted to find out what exactly had happened between Jezebel and Colin the night of his murder. Hopefully, the video evidence would finger the killer for certain, but my anxiety dictated I explore every angle to uncover the truth and protect Darla.

CHAPTER 10

The second I stepped into Tip 'Em Back, Jezebel yelled, "We're closed!" Her threatening tone of voice didn't leave much room for argument, and I almost turned and headed right back out the door. However, my need for information kept me in place, so I slipped off my sunglasses and shoved them in my bag. I wouldn't be intimidated by the woman. Well, I was, but I'd try to pretend I wasn't.

After my eyes to adjusted to the dim light, I glanced around searching for her. "Jezebel?" I called when I didn't find her.

"Is that you, Bernie?"

"Yes!"

She rounded the corner from the office, wiping her hands on a towel. Wearing a tank top that read, *Those are my workout words,* and shorts, her muscles bulged in her arms and legs as she walked. "What are you doing here? We don't have a class today, do we?"

"No." *Thank goodness.* "I wanted to talk to you for a few minutes." I hoped she wouldn't kick me out.

"Is Ruby here?"

I nodded, hoping my ghost would be my ticket to Jezebel sitting down with me.

Her mouth cracked into a large grin. "Hey, Ruby! You're the reason God invented the middle finger!"

Ruby snickered while I considered the insult. She may not be wrong on that one.

"Jezzy, you're more disappointing than an unsalted pretzel."

I relayed the message and both burst out laughing. "How I wish I could give that old bat a big hug," Jezebel said, shaking her head. "I miss her almost as much as I miss my own grandmother."

"I miss you too, honey," Ruby said. "I miss Janis as well."

Jezebel turned to me. "What did you need, Bernie? I'm in the middle of accounting, which I hate, so my mood's on the south end of foul."

"I wanted to talk to you about what happened the night you called the cops."

She furrowed her brow in confusion, and I guessed she was trying to recall *which* time she'd phoned the police. Tip 'Em Back was the dive bar on the outskirts of town, a magnet for unsavory characters.

"Oh! You mean that dirtbag who hit on me and ended up dead?"

"Yes. That's him."

"Sure! Come on in and belly up to the bar. I'll give you a blow-by-blow of what happened. Anything to escape accounting."

I followed her to the bar and pulled out a stool while she went around to the other side. "Do you want something?" she asked as she popped open a bottle of beer. The lid clanked to the floor.

"Just some water, please."

Jezebel chugged half her beer, then set it

down and pulled a glass off the shelf. I noted her tattoo-covered bicep flexed as she worked the water tap. "Here you go," she said, setting it down in front of me. "Why do you want to know about that night?"

"They're investigating the murder and I'm trying to get a timeline on where that guy was and what he did. I'm just looking for information."

Jezebel picked up her beer and stared at me as she finished it off. "Are you getting yourself tangled up in the murder investigation?"

"No. I'm trying really hard not to. My friend Darla also had a run in with him, and she's... she's scared. I'm trying to put her mind at ease with information."

"Are you hoping I'd say something that'll make me seem guilty?"

"N-no! Of course not!" I said, horrified she'd think that way.

"Then let the police do their jobs," Jezebel said. "If your friend is innocent, she's got nothing to worry about."

I couldn't explain that Darla's mental illness gave her a good case of paranoia and more anxiety than even I carried. That was her business and not mine to share.

"Can you tell me what happened that night?" I asked again, hoping she wouldn't question my motives further.

"Sure. The idiot came in here and sat in that very stool. I could tell he'd been drinking, but I served him anyway. I probably shouldn't have, but I did. He had two shots of whisky then nursed a beer."

"Did he say anything while he was here?"

Jezebel pulled back her long blonde hair and piled it up on top of her head with a rubber band. I winced, thinking it would hurt when she took it out. If I had an extra scrunchie on me, I would have offered it to her. "Yeah, he ran his mouth almost the whole time he sat there. He said women were awful beasts, he hated them all, and he'd never trust another one in his life."

I rolled my eyes and shook my head. "Did he also mention that he cheated on his fiancée and she broke off the engagement? That he was supposed to get married in two weeks?"

"No, he left out that part," Jezebel said,

chuckling. "I should have figured his anger stemmed from something like that. Typical man. It's always the woman's fault they can't keep their pants zipped. After his tirade about how horrible women are, he then proceeded to hit on me."

"What did he say?"

"That I was pretty but I looked like I needed a special kind of man to satisfy me. He informed me that he was up for the job. Then he asked for my phone number and where I lived. He wanted to meet up after I closed the bar."

"That's bold."

"I thought so, too," Jezebel replied with a chuckle. "I politely declined his enticing invitation."

Who could blame her?

"What happened then?"

"Well, after I told him I wouldn't be joining him for a night of passion, he began trolling around the bar looking for someone who would. Most of the women who come in here just want to be left alone. Most brushed him off nicely, but he became more agitated." Jezebel pointed across the room to the jukebox. "She was over there, minding her own business, dancing by herself. The next thing I knew, that jerk had her pinned up against the wall and was kissing her."

Adam hadn't mentioned anything about this turn of events. "Did you tell the police about the incident?"

"No. She asked me to leave her out of it, so I did. She was fine and didn't want to tangle with the cops."

A chill went down my spine and I outwardly shivered as I imagined a stranger assaulting me like that. "I take it the woman wasn't too happy about it?"

"She was angry, but not as furious as me. Stuff like that doesn't fly in my bar. I run a hassle-free zone for everyone."

"I can appreciate that. What did you do?" Although I already knew, I wanted to hear Jezebel's side of things.

She opened another beer. "I ran over, grabbed him by the back of the shirt, and yanked him off her. He tried to fight me, but he was too unsteady, so I ended up dragging him out the front door into the parking lot.

He finally staggered to his feet and we had a few words."

"Like what?"

Jezebel shrugged. "He called me a bunch of nasty names, then took a swing at me."

I pursed my lips together as Ruby laughed. "That was a mistake," she said.

"And you hit him?"

"Oh, yeah," she said. "I pounded that boy's face." She held out her hand where I noted the bruised knuckles. Pointing to a deep cut on one of her fingers, she muttered, "That's from his teeth."

"Jeez. Did he have any left?" Ruby asked. Goosebumps traveled over my back, so I knew she was right behind me looking over my shoulder.

"Ruby was wondering if he left here with any teeth," I said.

"As far as I know. I didn't find any in the parking lot, but I really didn't search that hard, either."

"Have you had your hand seen by a doctor?" I asked. "I mean, there could be all sorts of bacteria in the cut if it's from his mouth. The skin was broken."

Jezebel shook her head. "Nah. Soap and water always does the trick. I'll keep an eye on it though."

"She's probably got rabies," Ruby murmured, and I didn't disagree, but decided to keep the thought to myself.

"What happened after the fistfight?"

"I called the dirtbag a cab and threw him in myself. A while later, I called the cops, thinking I better file a report in case he decided to whine to the police about how a woman rearranged his face."

"The next day as I was leaving our session, I saw the police cruiser arrive," I said. "What did the sheriff have to say?"

"He asked me about that night, where I was after I closed up, who was with me, who could vouch that I didn't kill the guy... stuff like that."

I found it interesting Jezebel didn't seem the least bit rattled by Sheriff Walker's visit. Nothing like Darla, who was on the verge of a mental breakdown. Was it because Darla had a mental illness, or was Jezebel simply so untroubled by everything she simply didn't care?

After taking a long sip of water, I asked, "So you're aware you're a suspect, right?"

"Oh, sure," Jezebel said, tipping back her bottle. "I don't have an alibi for after I closed the bar. I went home by myself." She finished off her beer. "I'm never going to be able to get back to the accounting after these beers. I'd make all sorts of mistakes. Not that I mind, though."

I made errors while dead sober, so I understood her stance. But back to the murder. "Jezebel, why aren't you concerned that your name's been connected to a murder investigation?"

"Because I didn't do it."

Staring at my new friend, I became confused. Could she really have that much trust in the justice system? Didn't she ever read about the people who spent decades in prison for crimes they didn't commit?

"You're staring at me all weird," she said.

"People go to prison all the time for stuff they didn't do."

"Yes, that's true," Jezebel said. "But being on the police radar for this one isn't a huge deal to me. I know I beat the guy senseless, and I'll fully admit that. But I didn't kill him. I called him a cab and watched him get into it. I never saw him again."

"The sheriff sounds like he thinks you might have," I said.

Jezebel shrugged. "I think he told me that guy was killed with a knife. Is that right? I wasn't listening very well."

I nodded.

"Yeah, see, here's the thing, Bernie. If I had any intention of killing the guy, I never would have called the cops after I used his face as a punching bag. I would have let him go on his way, then circled back and did him in. He wouldn't have seen me coming."

"She's got some valid points," Ruby admitted.

"So you think because you beat up Colin and called the police, it exonerates you?"

"Maybe? To me, it does. I fully admit there was an altercation and that I laid hands on the man. Why would I call the cops if I had plans to kill him?"

Oddly enough, her argument made sense to me, but maybe it shouldn't.

"Thanks for your time, Jezebel," I said. "I really appreciate it."

"Sure! See you soon for a butt-kicking?"

I nodded and waved as I left the bar, the sun blinding me as I stepped outside. Hopefully I wouldn't receive a butt-kicking, but actually be able to give one... or at least to defend myself.

As I fished through my bag for my sunglasses, Ruby asked, "What do you think? I say she's not guilty."

"Perhaps," I muttered, climbing into the car. "But here's the thing: maybe after the cops left, she decided to take matters into her own hands and went to the hotel to kill him."

"And she thinks the fact she made the phone call protects her?"

"Maybe. It's like she's throwing it out there as cover. You know what I mean? She's admitting to hurting him and calling him a cab, but nothing else."

"I don't think she did it," Ruby said, shrugging. "She's strong enough, she's got the guts to do it, but I can't see her wasting her time with the jerk. She knocked his face in for messing with someone in her bar. After the last punch landed and she put him in a cab, I can't imagine her giving him a second thought, let alone planning out a murder."

When I compared Jezebel to Darla, they both had similar motives. Each had a drunk, obnoxious man in their establishments, and he offended both of them. Yet, they were the opposite ends in disposition. It was like comparing a tiger with a newborn puppy... one could be a raging beast, the other a docile innocent.

The fact that Jezebel definitely possessed the strength—both mentally and physically —to stick a knife in someone's chest was exactly why she needed to be kept on the list of suspects.

CHAPTER 11

*T*he next morning, I was having coffee with Amy and Cathy while they munched on the donuts I'd bought from Canyon Coffee. Now that we'd all gotten to know each other a little better, there was a friendship budding between us. Even Cathy, who tended to let Amy do the talking for her, participated fully in the conversations.

Although Cathy tried to keep Amy's spirits up, an aura of sadness still surrounded her. And rightfully so. Yes, she'd found out her fiancé had cheated on her, but she also loved him and now he was dead. She'd suffered a great loss, and frankly, if she had been the one to kill him, I'd be shocked.

Which meant the killer was still at large and two of my close friends—Darla and Jezebel—were being scrutinized for the murder. The idea of either one being responsible upset me greatly. I worried for them both. No matter how hard I tried not to think about the situation and allow the truth to unfold through the police investigation, the anxiety never left me for more than a few moments. I felt I had to do something to put the case to bed, not only for Darla's mental health, but for my own. I'd lost too much sleep with all my fretting and running different scenarios through my mind. What I could do, I had no idea.

As I laughed at something Cathy said, my phone buzzed in my pocket. I retrieved it and glanced at the screen. A reservation had been made. My guest would be arriving within the hour if I okayed it. I did just that and stood.

"I've got someone checking in fairly soon," I announced. "I need to look at the room and make sure everything is all right for them."

"Sure," Cathy said. "We'll entertain ourselves for a bit."

"They better be cool and not ruin our vibe here," Amy said. "Maybe they'll just keep to themselves and mind their own business."

My hope for each and every guest who walked through my door.

"Can we get in a sunset yoga session again?" Cathy asked. "That was so nice the other night."

"Sure," I replied, happy to lead them through another class. "For now, there's more coffee in the kitchen if you want it."

"Thanks, Bernie," they said in unison.

Before heading to the guest room, I stopped at the closet and grabbed the cleaning bucket. As I climbed the stairs, Ruby appeared at the top. "When can we go see Ned again?"

I strode through her and didn't answer until I was inside the guest room... or the Death Room as Ruby liked to refer to it. "I don't know. I suppose we'll wait for Adam to phone."

"Or you could be proactive and call him yourself," she suggested.

"He's busy solving a murder. He'll be in touch when he has time."

"Your patience is annoying."

"So is your restlessness."

"Bernie, I'm dead. I've got nothing to do and all the time in the world to do it. Of course I'm restless."

I turned to my grandmother, now exasperated myself. "I'm sorry, Ruby. If I knew how to send you to your final resting place, I would."

Her gaze narrowed and she crossed her arms over her chest. "Really?"

Suddenly realizing how my statement sounded, I tried to backtrack. "I... I just meant that I hate seeing you like this. I know you aren't happy. If there was something I could do to help you, I would."

"You could call Adam and we could go see Ned. And, I don't think that's what you meant at all. I think you wish I was gone. For good."

"Ruby, I—"

"Your wish is my command."

She slowly faded away, still glaring at me. With a sigh, I stared at the spot where she'd stood for a long time. Did I want Ruby gone, never to be seen again? I wouldn't lie... sometimes, yes. Most times, I loved having her around, even though she drove me crazy. When she showed herself again, I'd have to apologize for what I'd said.

But back to the task at hand. I couldn't stand in the middle of the Death Room staring at the carpet all day. Ruby and I had fought before and she always returned. She had nowhere else to go and didn't like spending much time alone. She'd be back soon.

No one had been in the room since I had done the deep cleaning, so I didn't see anything out of place. A quick dusting was in order, but that would be the extent of it. After setting down the bucket by the doorway, I grabbed a cloth and some oil, then rubbed down the desk, the dresser, and the bedframe. I also checked the bathroom one last time. Satisfied everything was in order,

I gathered my supplies and left the room, closing the door behind me.

Downstairs I found two coffee cups in the sink and the silence indicating I was home alone. Amy and Cathy must have slipped out for a walk or went to run errands. I sat down at the dining room table and took a moment to appreciate the quiet and calm my mind. Shutting my eyes, I tried to halt the continuous stream of questions about the murder and the worrying thoughts. After a few moments, I cursed and gave up. My busy brain wouldn't find any peace until the killer was behind bars.

Just as I placed my cleaning bucket back in the closet, the door chimes jingled. I hurried through the house to the front door. A woman with black hair down to her mid-back stood in the entryway, a suitcase at her side. As I approached her, I pegged her to be in her late twenties to early thirties. Her jeans and sweatshirt sagged off her thin body. With the lines on her face and her haunted gaze, I immediately guessed she was someone who'd had a rough go in life.

"Hi," I said, quickly wiping my hand on

my pants before offering it to her. "I'm Bernie, the owner."

She took my hand in hers and smiled. "Jessica. Thanks for taking my reservation so quickly. There's a metaphysical retreat beginning today and I had to leave the hotel. They didn't have any room for me. All the hotels are full. I feel lucky to have found you."

"Glad I could help you out," I said. Something bothered me about the woman, but I couldn't place what it was. Did I know her from somewhere? She seemed a bit familiar. "Come on over and let's get you checked in."

I led her to the desk in the corner of the room and pulled out the iPad. "If you could please fill this out."

"Sure, thanks."

"How long will you be staying?" I asked.

"Two nights, minimum," she replied, tapping the screen. "Maybe more. Will that be okay? Or will I have to find another place?"

My phone buzzed in my pocket. After pulling it out, I glanced at the screen. Someone inquiring about a room, but I was officially full so I declined the reservation and hung out my virtual *No Vacancy* sign. "Yes. The room is yours for as long as you need it."

Glancing around the living room, I searched for Ruby. Usually, she enjoyed checking out our new guests, but she was nowhere to be found. Probably still angry at me for my earlier comment.

"Is there anyone else staying here?" the woman asked.

"Yes. We have two other women. We're officially full."

"I hope they're quiet," she muttered, handing me back the iPad and her credit card. "I really need to get some rest."

I smiled as I tallied up the total, then ran the card. "They've been here a few days and they're both very nice." *Except one might be a murderer, but the jury's still out on that.*

Once I'd taken care of the check-in, I launched into my welcome spiel. "Breakfast, which consists of donuts and coffee, is served at seven. In the late afternoons, I also offer a yoga class on the back deck as the sun sets. You're free to join if you'd like.

Will you be doing any sightseeing while in town?"

She shook her head. "No. I'm here on family business."

"Well, if you get a chance and want to see the desert and surrounding area, I highly recommend Jumping Jack's Jeep Tours."

"Thank you."

I motioned toward the staircase. "I'll take you up to your room now."

She picked up her suitcase and followed me up the stairs. I fully expected Ruby to appear and make some wisecrack as I opened the door to the Death Room, but she remained hidden.

I stepped to the side so my guest could enter. "Here you go. If you need an extra blanket or pillow, they're in the closet. Extra toilet paper is under the sink, as well as more towels. If you need anything else, please don't hesitate to ask."

"Thank you," she murmured, glancing around and giving me her first smile. "This is so homey. I'm really glad I found you."

"Me, too. Enjoy your stay, and if you

want to join me for sunset yoga, please let me know. I'll slip my number under the door in a bit and you can text me if I'm not around."

"Sounds great."

I waved and exited the room, something still niggling at me. Had I met her before? I didn't think so. Perhaps I'd seen her around town?

The front door opened just as I reached the bottom of the stairs. Cathy and Amy had returned, each carrying a grocery bag.

"Hey!" Amy said. "We're going to make pancakes if that's okay with you. I've got a craving for chocolate chip."

I nodded and smiled, but a wave of guilt washed through me. I wished I still served breakfast for my guests, but it was for the best that I didn't. I didn't want to make anyone sick, and with me yielding a spatula, that was an excellent possibility. "Help yourself to the kitchen." The three of us filed through the dining room. "We've got a new guest. She's looking for some peace and quiet, so if you two could keep your voices down while in the hallway upstairs, I'd really appreciate it."

"Of course," Amy said, unloading the groceries onto the counter. "We'll be like little mice."

"Yuck," Cathy muttered.

"Do you want pancakes?" Amy asked while pointing at me.

"That sounds wonderful. Thank you."

As the two women took over my kitchen, I hurried into the living room and straightened up the couch pillows and magazines. I noted a few smudge marks on the coffee table, so I retrieved my furniture polish once again and gave the surface a quick scrub. I then moved into the dining room where I adjusted the chairs and shined the table.

When I returned to the kitchen, Amy was plating the pancakes.

"Those smell wonderful," I said, my mouth watering.

"Have a seat," she said. "It feels good to be doing something instead of worrying and crying."

I pulled out a stool and sat down as she slid a plate across the counter. Memories of Ruby taking me out to breakfast when I visited her as a little girl came to mind. She was never a good cook either, but we frequented a restaurant in town that served the best chocolate chip pancakes with whipped cream on top. Unfortunately, Plates of Pancakes wasn't in business any longer. My mother would have never allowed me such decadence as a morning meal. Fruit and fiber had been her rule of thumb, so my plate full of debauchery while visiting Ruby had always remained our little secret.

"These are delicious," I said between bites. "Absolutely amazing."

"She puts vanilla in them," Cathy said. "And heavy cream. Secret family recipe."

"Can I get in on those?" A voice from behind me said. "I can smell them upstairs."

I turned to find my new guest, and waved her in with a smile. "Sure. Come join us."

Glancing over at Cathy, I noted her furrowed brow as she stared at the woman. Amy's mouth hung open and I set down my fork. The air had changed and the silence had a vibe of trouble.

"If it's not okay, I'll go back upstairs," Jessica said.

"You're... you're her," Amy whispered. "Aren't you?"

"I swear it is," Cathy said.

"You're... are you Colin's sister?" Amy asked.

The color drained from Jessica's cheeks as I realized what had bothered me earlier. Jessica was the name Amy had used for Colin's sister. Oh, my word. Did I have Colin's sister staying with me?

The four of us traded glances for a long moment, then Jessica slowly nodded. "And what's your name again?"

"I'm... I'm Amy."

Jessica closed her eyes for a moment and shook her head. "Fantastic. Not only has my brother died, but I'm staying at the same place as the woman who committed the murder."

Uh-oh.

CHAPTER 12

"I didn't kill anyone!" Amy yelled as she fisted her hand at her side. "How dare you?"

"That's what the police say!" Jessica shouted. "The girlfriend most likely did it!"

"He cheated on me and I broke up with him! That doesn't mean I killed him!"

"You destroyed the last person in my family!"

Amy marched around the island with tears streaming down her cheeks heading directly for Jessica. Anger radiated off her in waves, her hands fisted at her sides. Cathy and I scrambled to our feet and placed ourselves between the two women. A fistfight in my kitchen? Not going to happen. I tried to recall if Jezebel and I had ever practiced how to break up a bout of fisticuffs, and nothing came to mind.

Cathy laid her hands on Amy's shoulders. "Take some deep breaths," she said. "Try to calm down. Getting hysterical isn't going to diffuse this weird situation."

What a perfect description.

Amy stared at her friend and did as instructed. After a moment, she glared at Jessica again. "Why are you even here?"

So many questions swirled through my mind. Cathy had insinuated that Jessica had disappeared once she graduated from high school and that Colin had thought she'd been on drugs. And now she stood in my kitchen?

Jessica sneered. "I'm here because the police called me and told me my brother had been murdered. I'm needed to take care of his remains."

"How did they track you down?" Amy asked. "You haven't been heard from in over a year."

"Why does it matter how they found

me?" Jessica shot back.

"You're right. It doesn't. It's so fitting that you didn't talk to your family for years except when you wanted money and now you're here after Colin's death."

"I don't think this is a good place for me to stay," Jessica said through gritted teeth. "I don't like the idea of being in the same building as the woman who murdered my brother."

"And I don't like the idea of staying in the same building as a selfish druggie!" Amy shouted as Jessica retreated from the room.

I honestly didn't know what to do. Go after Jessica? Stay in the kitchen and find out more information from Amy and Cathy? And where the heck was Ruby? All this yelling should have summoned her like a moth to a flame.

"How did you recognize her?" I asked when the door upstairs slammed shut.

"She seemed vaguely familiar to me," Cathy said. "I now remember seeing pictures of her at Colin's house when we dated in high school."

"I've met her once," Amy grumbled.

"About a year ago, she crawled out from under her rock and came to Phoenix, asking Colin for money. He told her he wouldn't fuel her drug habit. They had a huge screaming match at his place while I was there. They said horrible things to each other."

Jessica appeared a bit gaunt but she seemed to have her wits about her. Was she on drugs? It certainly didn't seem that way. "Perhaps she's cleaned herself up?" I offered.

"Maybe," Amy said, shrugging. "She wasn't nice to me a year ago, and I can see she still doesn't like me."

As Amy burst into tears and Cathy enveloped her in a big hug, I heard footsteps on the staircase. Hurrying into the living room, I found Jessica heading for the front door with her suitcase in tow.

"Jessica, I'm... I'm so sorry."

She turned to me. "It's not your fault. You couldn't have known."

"You're right. I didn't."

She bit her bottom lip and stared at me for a long moment before speaking. "I don't know why I feel the need to explain myself to you, but I do. I cut myself off from my family after high school because of abuse from my father... He used to sneak into my room in the middle of the night. Colin never knew about it. To cover the pain, I did a lot of drugs... and I did things to get those drugs that I'm not proud of. But I've been clean for just over a year. I've been working through my trauma with a counselor and part of that is—was—making amends with Colin. I hated him for a long time because he escaped my father." Tears sprung to her eyes. "Amy didn't want me to have anything to do with Colin. She was nothing but toxic and rude to me when I saw him a year ago. I gave him space because of her. And now... now I have so many regrets."

"I'm sorry," I whispered as the tears tracked down her cheeks. My chest hurt at the horror of her abuse and the agony it must have caused.

I also noted the discrepancies in stories between Jessica's and Amy's. Each said the other had been the cause of the issues at their last meeting. The truth always lay somewhere in the middle of a two-sided tale, and I had to believe that neither were innocent when it came to bad behavior.

"The police think she did it," Jessica said, pointing to the kitchen. "They're expecting security footage from the hotel at any moment. An arrest is imminent, Bernie. They'll be coming for her."

She dragged her suitcase toward the door as I recalled her saying the hotels were all full due to the metaphysical retreat.

"Where are you going?" I asked. "Where will you stay?"

"I'll figure something out," she said. "I can sleep in my car if need be. God knows I've slept in worse places."

"If you decide you want to come back, I'll hold your room," I blurted, regretting the words the second they hung in the air between us. I had just turned down another reservation. If business had been slow, my offer would have been okay. But I had people who wanted to stay with me and I could always use more money. However, being a decent human was more important. Perhaps she needed some time to cool off and she'd regret her decision to leave.

"Don't worry about it," Jessica called, heading to her car. "I won't darken your doorstep again. Not with *her* staying here."

I walked out to the pathway and watched until she drove away and rounded the corner out of sight. The poor woman had had a rough life and I couldn't help but feel bad for her, but I also admired her ability to turn herself around. With all the baggage to unpack, it must not have been easy.

With a sigh, I returned to the house, shut the door behind me, and hurried back to the kitchen. The sight of the pancakes turned my stomach, even though the drama was the cause of my discomfort.

"She won't be back," I announced as I sat down on my stool and pushed the plate away.

"I'm so sorry, Bernie," Amy said, reaching across the counter and squeezing my hand. "The woman is bad news, so it's probably for the best."

"Did you know she's cleaned herself up?" I asked. "She says she's no longer on drugs."

Amy's brow furrowed and she shook her

head. "No. Like I said, I haven't seen her in just over a year. Colin never mentioned anything recently about her either."

"Looks like she's going to get the whole estate," Cathy mused, shoving a forkful of pancakes into her mouth.

"The estate?" I asked.

Amy nodded. "Colin's family was very wealthy. When his parents died, he discovered they'd completely cut out Jessica from the will unless she could prove she'd gotten her life together."

I understood why they'd done it—a drug addict shouldn't be given large sums of money. But I bet the slight hurt Jessica on a very deep personal level, especially after suffering such abuse from her father.

"How wealthy were they?" I asked, more curious than anything.

"Multi-millions," Amy replied. "Jessica will never have any financial worries again."

Money was always a great motive for murder. Had Jessica killed her brother for control of the estate? It sounded perfect in theory, but there was one problem: how would she know he was in Sedona? From what I gathered, Colin and Jessica hadn't talked in ages. It didn't seem like normal behavior for him to call his sister and complain about his fiancée leaving him while explaining he was driving to Sedona to try to rescue the relationship.

No, that didn't make any sense at all.

"I wonder how long she's been here," Amy said. "Maybe her plan had been to kill Colin in Phoenix, but then she followed him up here?"

Interesting how her line of thought followed mine.

"That doesn't make sense," Cathy said.

"None of it does," Amy said. "I still don't understand why Colin's dead. Who would do such a thing?"

"Well, it will be over soon," I replied. "Jessica says the police are closing in with more evidence."

"That's good. I want justice for Colin." Tears trickled down Amy's face once again. "I can't believe he's gone."

As I began gathering up the dishes to set them in the dishwasher, I couldn't help but ponder if Amy would have gotten back together with Colin. Perhaps he would have just needed to grovel a bit more? Buy a bigger bouquet of flowers? She was obviously quite distraught, and I wondered if she regretted her decision to call off the wedding. Perhaps she had been trying to teach him a lesson by breaking off the relationship but had every intention of marrying him even thought she'd said otherwise.

I glanced around searching for Ruby. Usually, she'd be listening and commenting on everything, but she'd been radio silent. Was she sitting in her tunnel, pouting? Had I really hurt her feelings that badly?

"I'm going upstairs," Amy murmured. "I'm suddenly absolutely exhausted."

"I'll head up with you," Cathy replied. "Drama can be so draining."

When I heard both bedroom doors shut, I whispered, "Ruby!"

I waited for a moment for her to show herself, then hurried into my own bedroom and closed the door.

"Ruby!" I hissed. "Come out!"

Fully expecting her to appear behind me

and attempt to scare me to death, I braced myself while glancing over my shoulder. Nothing.

"I'm sorry, Ruby!" I said, keeping my voice low. "I shouldn't have said what I did. Of course I want you around. You and I need to talk! Please come out!"

Silence.

"Ruby!"

Slowly sitting down on my rocking chair, I glanced around the space once more, expecting her to appear lying across my yellow comforter. My cat, Elvira, came out from under the bed and hopped on my lap. She quickly curled up and began to purr as I stroked her head. The fact she had chosen to spend time with me meant that Ruby truly wasn't anywhere around. Elvira always preferred being with my ghost.

I really wanted to hash out all the new information with Ruby. Was she that upset with me? Or... I gasped. What if she'd been able to go to her final resting place? And she hadn't said goodbye? I couldn't imagine moving forward with her anger and our argument being the last memory of her.

THE FIANCÉ IS FINISHED

"Ruby?" The silence of the house hung around me like an old, wet moldy blanket, suffocating me. I wanted to hear Ruby's chatter and laughter. "I'm sorry," I whispered.

My phone buzzed in my pocket and I groaned as I pulled it out. I had too much going through my mind to deal with anyone. The possibility of a murderer under my roof—or one who'd just left—my missing ghost, the worry for Darla... I couldn't focus with it all spinning around in my busy brain.

"Hi, Jack," I said, my gaze flickering around the room. If anything would bring Ruby out, it was Mr. Dimples calling.

"Everything okay?" he asked. "You sound like you've had it for the day and it's not even noon."

"I'm pretty close." Where the heck had my ghost gone?! "It feels like it should be bedtime."

"Well, I hate to heap more on you, but we've got a situation with Darla."

"Oh, no! What happened?"

CHAPTER 13

"Well, have you heard about the murder at the Sedona Grand Hotel?" Jack asked.

"Of course. I have a suspect staying with me."

"Seriously? Isn't that dangerous?"

"You would think so, but so far, no. She seems pretty harmless. Heartbroken. I honestly don't think she did it."

"Who is it?"

"The girlfriend. Amy Parsons is her name. She's staying here with her friend, Cathy. Is Darla okay?"

Jack sighed and I imagined him sitting in his small office with his work boots covered in red Sedona dust up on his desk. "For now. The police were at the diner a while ago asking her some follow-up questions. She came over ranting and crying after they left."

I groaned and shook my head. "What did she say?"

"One minute she was sobbing, then next minute she was threatening to blow up the police station. A lot of incoherent things. I'm afraid she's going to have another... what are they called? Episode? A break?"

Oh, my word. Darla shouldn't be voicing such things. "Did anyone hear her threaten to blow up the police station?"

"No. It's just me and business is dead. I'm not even supposed to be here today."

"Why is that?"

"The guy who was killed booked a Romantic Rendezvous Tour with me. Said he was going to win back his fiancée no matter what he had to do."

I'd never heard of the Romantic Rendezvous Tour. "Is that something new? Where do you take them?"

"We go the usual route, but then I stop

down by the creek and lay out a picnic for them. Champagne, sandwiches, and a couple of brownies from Canyon Coffee. Lynn, the high school music teacher, plays violin for them while they lounge by the creek and eat. She's really talented. It's hard to believe she's not in some big-time orchestra. It's an all-day thing."

Which also meant it was very expensive but nothing a multi-millionaire's wallet couldn't handle.

"It sounds nice," I said. Maybe I could snag a friends and family discount and take Adam when all this was over.

"Yeah, it is. But getting back to Darla, is there any way you can convince Adam to tell her she's not going to prison for the rest of her life? She's got a huge case of paranoia. If we could ease her mind about the investigation, she'd be in a much better place."

"Well, let me call and find out. I'll phone you right back." I disconnected Jack and dialed Adam.

"Hey, Bernie," Adam answered with a sigh. "It's not a good time."

"I'm sorry to bother you, but I was wondering if you would please swing by Darla's and tell her she's not a suspect. I understand you have your proof of who killed Colin."

"Not true," Adam replied. "I'm supposed to have it in the next couple of hours or so. I can't tell Darla anything until we've gone through all the evidence."

I rubbed my forefinger over my temple and shut my eyes as a headache began to form. "Adam—"

"An arrest will be made when we're ready. Not before."

"But Darla's in a bad place and extremely concerned she's going to go to prison for a crime she didn't commit. She needs some sort of assurance before she loses it."

"Look. I understand you're worried about her but the fact of the matter is that she had motive and she had opportunity. I can't rule her out. Colin went to her restaurant, acted like a drunk jerk and stiffed her. She has no alibi for that night after she closed. Her knife set matches the murder weapon."

Recalling Jezebel's theory, I asked, "Why

would she call the cops and report him if she was going to kill him?"

"I don't know, Bernie! People do stupid stuff every single day!"

"But—"

"No buts about it, Bernie. Look, I have to go. Ned has decided we're playing a game of hide-and-go-seek and I can't find my notebook."

We'd discovered Ned's existence when he'd thrown a book at Ruby while she insulted him until he revealed himself, but it had hit me square in the forehead. None of us understood why he had the ability to manipulate objects while my ghost couldn't pick up a toilet scrubber to help me clean. Ned's deep guffaws permeated the background. Obviously, he was quite pleased with his little joke and for the first time, I was glad Adam couldn't hear or see his ghost. If he hadn't sounded so angry, I would have laughed. "Ruby hasn't been a good influence."

"No. Not at all. I think I liked it better when Ned minded his own business and left me alone. I'll talk to you later."

I pursed my lips together and called Jack.

"What did he say?"

"That he's supposed to receive the evidence at some point in the next hour or so, but he won't say anything to Darla until they're certain who committed the crime."

"Oh, man." Jack sighed. "Honestly, I worry she's not going to make it that long. In fact, she just closed up the diner." Jumping Jack Jeep Tours was right next door to Darling's Diner, so he had a bird's-eye view of everything she did.

"It's the middle of the day," I said, turning my phone to speaker and setting it on my dresser.

"I know. I wish there was a way we could see the evidence. I get that Adam's following protocol, but our friend is on a sinking ship."

An idea began to form, but I quickly brushed it aside. "It's too bad we can't get into Adam's place and snoop around when he's not there. Maybe we would find evidence to put Darla's mind at ease."

Jack was quiet a long time. So long I

wondered if we'd lost the connection. "Jack?"

"Sorry. I was just thinking. You may have something there."

"What's that?"

"Breaking into Adam's condo."

I snorted and shook my head. "I'm not a locksmith and I don't have a key. Besides, I'd feel pretty bad about doing that to my boyfriend."

"All we need to do is figure out when he's not going to be home. He'll never know we were there. We could really save Darla a lot of worry and possibly prevent a complete breakdown."

He had a point. Darla slipping into a schizophrenic episode wouldn't do anyone any good. In fact, she could lose everything if she had to close the diner for another long stretch of time like she'd done before. Darla had admitted to me she was barely hanging on both mentally and financially.

"Do you remember a couple of months ago when I told you I've done things in my past I'm not proud of?" Jack asked.

"Yes."

"This is between you and me, Bernie." My heart thundered when I realized he would reveal a big secret. But did I want to be enlightened? I liked Jack. I liked our friendship. I didn't want that to change and hoped the new information wouldn't cause a fissure in our relationship.

"Okay," I whispered, completely torn between curiosity and blissful ignorance.

"If we want to get into Adam's place, I can do it. I... I uh... used to be a burglar. I spent some time in prison for it in my former life."

I gasped and stared at my phone, unable to believe what I'd just heard. A burglar? Prison? *Jack?* My goodness, he hadn't been kidding when he'd told me he had a dark past. When considering those who had done time in prison, visions of angry men covered in tattoos came to mind, not sunny, good-natured, handsome men with dimples like Jack. A very potent reminder that a person shouldn't be judged by looks.

Once my initial shock had passed, curiosity took over. "What... what happened? How did you get caught?"

Jack chuckled. "We'll talk about it some other time. We've got more important things to worry about than my bad life decisions."

"You can't leave me hanging like this!" I yelled. "Give me the brief version."

"Fine. I had a guy who worked as a valet at one of the priciest restaurants in Portland, Oregon. When someone pulled up in a fancy car, he'd call me, read off their address from the paperwork in the glove compartment, and I'd hit their place. We kept the gig up for a couple of years until one guy had a dog who pinned me in the laundry room on top of the washer until its owner arrived home. That thing was a huge Rottweiler, mean as all get out... frothing at the mouth, lunging at me with open jaws. Scared the heck out of me. Never heard or saw the darn thing until he was right behind me."

"So you ran into the laundry room? Why not out the door?"

"I got turned around in the house. I thought I was headed for the back door, but instead it was the laundry room. Total rookie move. I shut the door between us, but he eventually took that down. I swear that thing was on steroids or something."

"You were lucky you weren't killed."

"I know. Even though I knew they'd cart me off to jail, I'd never been so happy to see the police."

"What about alarms?" I asked, truly fascinated by this new information. "How did you get around those?"

"Surprisingly, a lot of people don't set their alarms when they're leaving for short amounts of time."

"So you didn't have any James Bond gadgets to bypass them if they were on?"

"No. I kept things pretty simple. Just me and my lock picks. Can we get back to Darla? All this talk about my former life I'd rather forget is making me uncomfortable."

Right. My friend on the verge of a mental health breakdown.

"She needs proof she's not on the police radar, Bernie," Jack continued. "I feel like we're on a race against time with her."

Adam had said that he expected the file footage from the hotel at any time. I knew he was at home. If he left his condo, Jack and I could enter and I could look at the computer for a few moments. Once I had visual confirmation of who had killed Colin, Jack and I could put Darla's mind at ease and hopefully avoid another schizophrenic break.

But burglarizing Adam's place left a horrible taste in my mouth. I would not only be breaking the law, but as his girlfriend, Adam was supposed to *trust* me. It was a complete violation. But if he never found out, Jack and I would be the only ones aware of what we'd done. He wasn't going to tell anyone, and I could keep a secret. I'd been hiding my ghost from almost everyone, except Adam.

"Bernie, if you decide you want to do this, I can't go inside with you," Jack said. "I'll get the lock open without any issues, but after that, you're on your own."

"I understand," I murmured. Gosh, this felt wrong on so many levels, not to mention dangerous. There was no way of me knowing if Adam was home or not without creeping around his condo and peering into the windows like some sort of stalker. Or, I could phone and casually ask where he was and what he was up to, but he seemed to be on the cranky side and my questions would only make things worse. He may not even answer.

"Hang on one second," Jack said. "I have to take this call."

I weighed my options in silence. Darla was in a horrible place. I wanted to help her, to give her what she needed to move forward in her recovery. The stress of the situation was becoming a huge setback for her. She seemed to be unraveling right before my eyes. All she wanted to know was that she wasn't a suspect in the murder any longer.

Understandably, Adam couldn't provide that information to her, or me, until he had all the evidence evaluated. But even then, would he share it? He wrongly seemed to believe I wanted to be involved with the investigation and he carried guilt from having me assist him on the last murder and almost dying. What Jack suggested was wrong, but was it right to allow Darla to suffer like she was?

Jack came back on the line. "I've got to go, Bernie. That was Darla's mom, Vicky."

"What's happening?"

"Darla called her and is really upset. Vicky asked me to check up on her."

"Oh, no."

"Yeah, we need to do something."

After he hung up, I stared at the phone and debated whether to call Adam again and beg him for information.

"Okay, I'm back," Ruby said, appearing on the bed. "You obviously can't pull this one off by yourself."

Elvira jumped from my lap and hurried over to the bed, curling up with my ghost.

Relief washed through me at the sight of my dead grandmother, despite my traitorous cat. She hadn't gone to her final resting place and I had the chance to make amends, unlike Jessica and Colin. The guilt weighed heavily on Jessica that she'd never been able to right her relationship with her brother. "Ruby, I'm sorry about earlier."

"Yeah, yeah." She waved her hand in front of her face. "Of course, the second I make my grand exit and vow to never show myself again, things get interesting around here."

"You've been listening?"

"How could I not with Amy and Jessica screaming in the kitchen like a couple of angry banshees? And Mr. Dimples revealing his dark side? Jeez, he gets sexier by the second."

"I don't know what to do, Ruby," I said, sighing. "Darla is in bad shape."

"Yes, I heard that as well. Frankly, I'm a bit irritated at the lover boy copper about this situation, but it's par for the course. Rule seven of life: cops will always annoy you."

"You see then what Jack is willing to do? To help me break in to Adam's condo?"

"Oh, yes. But that's dangerous for you. If you're caught, you're in trouble up to your armpits."

"Exactly."

She smiled and gave me a wink. "But I'm here now, Bernie, and I have a plan."

CHAPTER 14

*P*reviously when Ruby said she had a plan, I'd almost died. This time, I had to admit her idea seemed fairly safe. In fact, I didn't see how I could suffer any injuries unless I tripped over my own feet or a meteor landed on Adam's building while I was inside. Overall, I wasn't worried about bodily harm.

Emotional harm? That was another story. If Adam discovered I had violated his space, it could lead to the collapse of our relationship. But, I had a decision to make. Either I helped my friend avoid a complete mental breakdown or I took the chance of Adam discovering me.

"Piece of cake!" Ruby said, snapping her finger once she'd finished sharing the details. "He'll never know."

Which also bothered me. *I'd* know what I'd done, and I'd have to live with it.

I swung by Jumping Jack Jeep Tours to pick up the burglar. He grinned as he slid into the front seat and ran his hand through his brown hair, his green eyes gleaming with excitement.

"Hello, Mr. Dimples," Ruby purred from the back seat. "Aren't you looking sexy today? You've been a very, very bad boy, and I like it."

Oh, my goodness.

"Ready?" Jack asked. I noted the small black pouch he carried, which I assumed held the tools he'd used in his former life.

I nodded and sighed. "How's Darla?"

"She's resting."

I pulled out onto the main road and headed for Adam's.

Jack turned to me. "Bernie, I have to admit, I've missed this rush I used to get before a job."

If by rush he meant the curling of my

stomach as I fought nausea and the feeling of my heart pounding out the front of my chest, I'd gladly pass. "Well, I'm not happy we're doing this, but I feel there isn't a choice. And we have to for Darla's sake."

"You're sure he's working from home?" Jack asked.

I nodded. "That's what he said earlier."

"He'll either go back to the office or run out for coffee or something," Jack said. "I'm really confident about this."

"Were you confident the time the dog trapped you on top of the washing machine?"

"Yeah, I was," Jack replied, chuckling. "I thought things would go much smoother."

I didn't point out he could be wrong about our afternoon adventure and we could end up in a lot of trouble—both legally and on a more personal level with Adam.

"Ask Mr. Dimples what lucky woman he's dating these days," Ruby said from the backseat.

Jack wasn't aware of Ruby's existence, so

I bit my tongue to keep from answering her. He didn't date. He slept around, and I certainly didn't want to hear about those escapades. Ruby, however, would love nothing more.

We drove past Adam's complex and I spotted his police cruiser sitting in front of the building.

"He's here," Jack said, flexing his fingers. Apparently, burglars did warmup exercises?

I parked behind Adam's unit where he couldn't see my car and turned off the ignition with shaky fingers. "Stay here," I said. "Let me go check if he's around."

Jack wasn't aware, but this was the point in the plan where Ruby became very useful. I wouldn't have to peek in his windows, hoping he didn't catch me. Instead, I could stand just outside his front door and she would go in and inspect the condo, and hopefully talk to Ned.

Taking a deep breath, I moved slowly toward Adam's place. When I stood by the entrance, I motioned for her to head in. She ghosted through the door.

"Hey, Ned!" she yelled. "You around?"

Since Ruby couldn't go more than fifteen feet from me when we were outside our home, I overheard the conversation loud and clear.

"What are you doing here?" Ned asked. "Where's Miss Bernadette?"

How many times did I have to tell him I didn't need the formalities?

"She's outside. Is the copper around?"

"Yes, in fact he is. I do believe he's getting ready to leave, though. Why isn't Miss Bernadette coming in?"

"We don't want him to know we're here," Ruby explained. "It's a surprise."

Apparently, Ruby had decided Ned didn't need the truth, which was fine with me.

"I'm not particularly fond of surprises," he said, his voice holding a hint of hesitancy.

"That may be true, but you like to dabble in trouble. You tried to rob a bank. You're with us on this plan!"

Ned chuckled as Ruby yelled, "He's here,

Bernie! Coming out the front door in seconds!" She ghosted outside and pointed around the building. "Hide! Run like your butt's on fire!"

I hurried around the side, pressed my back against the wall, and crouched down behind a bush, aptly named the Catclaw. My sweatshirt caught on the thorns and I hissed as they dug into my skin.

Ruby stood on the other side of the plant. Through her ghostly form, I watched Adam drive away. Relief and dread swept through me at once. The great thing: the plan was working to perfection. The bad: I now had to break into my boyfriend's condo.

"Let's get the hottie," Ruby said. "It's go-time."

I ran back to my car and waved for Jack to follow me. He trailed behind me silently until we reached Adam's door, then he unzipped his pouch. I stared at the parking lot, keeping an eye out for Adam's return while Jack studied the lock. I prayed the neighbors would mind their own business.

Having someone call the cops while we were breaking into a cop's home? That had trouble written all over it.

"Look at his butt in those jeans," Ruby murmured as she stood next to me, facing Jack. "God made quite the creation there."

The difference between Ruby and me astounded me at times. While I sweated and fought nausea, she admired Jack's assets. The moment probably wouldn't have been much different if she were alive.

"It's done," Jack said quietly as I heard the click of the door opening. "I'll wait in the car. Do what you have to do."

I turned and stared at the cracked door, my stomach churning. No doubt, Adam would never be aware I was here. Yet, I was doing something very, very wrong. But I had to help Darla.

"Let's go!" Ruby said, walking through the door. "We're back, Ned!"

After taking a deep breath, I followed and shut the door behind me, my heart galloping so quickly, I leaned up against the wall to keep from passing out.

"What are you doing here, Miss

Bernadette?" Ned asked, appearing next to Ruby. "I didn't know you were coming. Adam didn't mention it."

"Like I told you, it's a surprise!" Ruby said. "Hurry up, Bernie."

Adam's laptop perched on the coffee table in the living room, surrounded by papers. I hurried over and sat down on the couch. After rubbing my sweaty palms on my jeans, I placed my hands on the keyboard and tapped the space bar. The black screen came alive and I typed in the password I'd seen him use many times.

Taking some deep breaths, I tried to focus as I wiped the beads of sweat from my forehead with my sweatshirt. Adam had been reading over Jezebel's police report. I scanned it quickly and saw nothing that contradicted what I already knew about her encounter with Colin. Paging through, I found Darla's statement. Nothing new there, either.

Ah… the statement from the man who had the confrontation with Colin in the bar. Mr. Grady.

I was minding my own business when this

young fellow sat down on the stool next to me. He ordered a couple of shots. Not sure what he was drinking, though. I was watching the game. He knocked over his beer and got me wet. Now, I was upset, but ready to let it go. Things happen. Except he started screaming at me that the mess was my fault, even though I was the one covered in beer. Then the guy took a swing at me, but thankfully, he missed. Hotel security showed up and kicked him out of the bar. Told him to go to bed. I went upstairs and changed, then returned to the bar. Never saw the jerk again.

Adam had highlighted the last sentence. I looked over his written papers and found a note. *Check into hotel security footage on Grady / bar / Grady returning to hotel room.*

So he was expecting video of not only the time leading up to the murder, but probably of the interaction between Grady and Colin.

Interesting, but it did nothing to clear Darla of any involvement.

I quickly glanced over Adam's email inbox, which was almost as boring as mine. An ad for car insurance. An email noting the landlord had received his rent payment. Another from a local hotel advertising their weekend specials.

"What are you looking for?" Ned asked, his brow furrowed. "I don't think I like you here without Adam present."

"Ned, I told you, it's fine," Ruby said. "You need to relax, old man."

"I'm trying to help a friend," I said, hoping to appeal to any soft side Ned may have. "I thought Adam may have the answer I need to set her mind at ease. She's... she's not well and is very upset. The stress only makes her condition worse."

"That's too bad. Why doesn't Adam help her?"

"Because he's a copper," Ruby said. "He's got to follow rules and protocols that the rest of us don't."

"He doesn't seem like a bad lawman," Ned said.

"He's not." I stood and walked over to the two ghosts. "Adam's a very good person and one that I care for very much. But I need to help my friend."

Ned stared at me a long time, then nodded. "I understand. Friendship can run deeper than family. I had that brotherly connection with my partner, Sam."

"You got shot because of him," Ruby said.

"Yes. But I hold no regrets or ill will any longer. He was a good man."

"Thank you for your understanding," I said, returning to the computer. After poking around a little longer, I concluded that either the hotel security footage hadn't been sent to Adam, or it was not on his computer, or I just couldn't find it. Maybe it had been stored behind the firewall of the sheriff's website?

I picked up a few other papers lying around and read them. Mostly, they consisted of notes Adam had jotted down regarding the case, but they didn't lead me to any information I could pass on to free Darla from her worry.

"There's nothing here," I said, glancing up at the ghosts. "Has he said anything to you, Ned? About the murder?"

The cowboy shook his head. "No, Miss Bernadette. Nothing direct that I can recall, although he's always muttering to himself while he slaves away on that there device." Ned pointed at the computer. "He's been staring at that thing for a long time today, like he was waiting for it to do something important."

"We better hit the road, Bernie," Ruby cut in. "Who knows where the copper went or when he's going to get back?"

"I know," I muttered, then glanced back to the computer, willing an email to come in. I clicked around a little more hoping I'd missed something, but then sighed. "You're right. We need to leave."

Just as I set down the laptop and stood, a little ding sounded and I quickly grabbed the computer and maneuvered to the email. Sedona Grand Hotel had sent Adam something.

"Oh, my word," I whispered as I opened it.

A video downloaded. My breath came in short spurts and the room suddenly became quite warm.

"What is it?" Ruby asked, hurrying over. "I can feel your anxiety. It's like a dang noose around my neck ready to choke the life out of me."

"Imagine how I feel." I stared at the screen. The hallway of the hotel came into view. I couldn't tell what floor it was, but they all looked alike and visions of being chased down one came back to haunt me. Goosebumps crawled over my skin as sweat broke out on my brow. Not the time for flashbacks. I had to concentrate.

The backside of a person wearing an oversized gray hoodie and jeans came into view. The figure strode down the hallway. I couldn't tell if it was a man or woman because of the bulk of the clothing.

They stopped outside the door and glanced to their right, then their left. The footage was so grainy, I couldn't make out a face under the hood, but I did note the hair hanging down the sides of their face and out the front of the sweatshirt.

The person knocked on the door. After a few seconds, it opened and they lunged forward. The panel shut behind them. I gasped, imagining what was happening to Colin as bile rose in my throat. Long moments passed while I stared at the screen, my heart thundering. When the door opened, the attacker once again surveyed the hallway, then rushed toward the camera. Blood stained the front of the gray sweatshirt.

"That's a woman," Ruby muttered. "Wish she'd look up, though. I can't see her face under the hood."

The video ended and I rewound it, then played it again. This time I stopped frame-by-frame and searched for any signs of recognition.

I found none. She must have known where the cameras were and kept her face hidden from the lens.

"We better go, Bernie," Ruby said.

After shutting down the video player and marking the original email as unread, I stood. "Have a good afternoon, Ned."

"Are you sure you two aren't up to something that's going to hurt Adam?" he asked.

Only if he discovers I was here.

"Of course not," Ruby said. "We'll see you soon, Old Timer."

I waited inside as Ruby ghosted through the door. "We're in the clear! The copper's nowhere to be seen." she yelled. "Come on out."

After shutting the panel behind me, I walked as quickly as possible back to my car hoping not to draw attention to myself. Ruby trailed behind me quietly.

"Did you find what you need?" Jack asked as I opened the door and slid inside.

I started the car and jammed the gear shift into reverse. "I think so."

"Is it going to put Darla's mind at ease?"

"Yes," I said, slamming the car into drive and turning out on to the main road.

"You better slow down there, speed racer," Ruby said from the back seat. "Last thing we need right now is a ticket or an accident."

She was right. I took some deep breaths and loosened my death grip on the steering wheel. I had to keep my focus on the goal: to help Darla. "The woman who killed Colin had black hair."

Jack turned to me. "How do you know? What did you find?"

"I saw security footage from the hotel. A woman went into his room, then came out with blood on the front of her sweatshirt. She had long black hair."

"That's definitely not Darla."

"No, it's not." In fact, I knew exactly who the killer was.

CHAPTER 15

*J*ack and I remained quiet as I drove back to Jumping Jack Jeep Tours. The weight of the violation of Adam's space weighed heavily on me and I kept reminding myself that he'd never find out. He couldn't see or hear Ned, so even if the ghost wanted to share what he'd witnessed, it would be impossible.

"We have to promise each other we won't tell Adam what we've done," Jack said. Obviously, the transgression bothered him as well and his thoughts traveled on the same wavelength as mine.

"I won't say a word," I muttered. "I feel awful about it."

"So do I, but we had to do it for Darla. So she doesn't have another breakdown. If the information helps put her mind at ease, that's what's important."

"You guys should make a blood pact," Ruby said. "You know, cut your palms and shake on the promise like they do in the movies."

I pulled into our destination and parked. Slicing open my hand and exchanging bodily fluids wasn't going to make me trust Jack any more than I already did.

"If he spills the beans, you can always knife him," Ruby said. "The other prisoners will understand if you're caught. They shank rats all the time."

And I wasn't going to physically knife Jack, no matter what he did. My grandmother watched too much television.

After I killed the engine, I sighed and closed my eyes while laying my head back on the headrest. Exhaustion flooded through me.

"Let's go see her," Jack said as he unbuckled his seatbelt. "She'll be happy with the news."

I nodded and exited the car. Ruby followed, humming a tune as if she didn't have a care in the world. Being dead, she didn't. I almost envied her... almost.

We walked over to the diner, which was still closed. A man and woman with two children stood outside and peered in through the windows.

"Do you work here?" the man asked when he noticed us approaching. "We hoped to grab some lunch."

Jack shook his head. "Unfortunately, the owner is sick so she had to close. We're personal friends checking in on her."

"That's too bad," the man said. "We heard the milkshakes here are great."

"I want one!" the younger child whined.

"You and me both, kid!" Ruby chimed in. "Chocolate and vanilla swirl would hit the spot."

Except Ruby couldn't eat or drink because she was dead.

"You may want to try back tomorrow," I said. "We're hoping she'll feel better by then. But in the meantime, Sarah's Smoothies is down the street a ways and they have great drinks as well."

"These people don't look like bovine," Ruby said. "Wheatgrass, lemongrass... it's cow food."

"The chocolate and peanut butter with whipped cream is one of my favorites," I continued. "The smoothie place isn't quite as good as the milkshakes here, but the treats hit the sweet spot."

I'd never admit it, but Sarah's Smoothies were the best in the state, as far as I was concerned. However, I wanted to help Darla and hopefully they'd remember what I said when the diner was open.

"We'll give it a try," the wife said, taking her younger child's hand. "Thanks for the tip!"

As they strode away, Jack and I went to the side of the building and up the rickety wooden staircase to Darla's apartment. The railing had once been white, but the paint had peeled in the Arizona sun. Another few weeks would be perfect painting weather, so I made a mental note to take on the job.

Maybe Adam and I could team up and knock it out in a day or two. Scraping the old paint would take the most time.

I glanced through the window as Jack knocked and found Darla lying on the couch while staring at the television. Her lips moved slightly, as though she were muttering to herself.

"This doesn't look good," I whispered as she rose from the sofa and I waved.

"Hey." She pulled open the door. "Come in, you guys!"

"How're you doing?" Jack asked.

Darla shuffled back over to the couch and collapsed, pulling the blankets over her again. Her cheeks had lost their rosy tint. She gathered her greasy blonde hair up into a bun, securing the strands with a scrunchie she grabbed from the coffee table. "Not too bad," she said. "Much better now the diner is closed. I just had too much on my mind to function."

I sighed in relief. She seemed much more stable than before. I noted a vase full of fresh flowers on the kitchen table. I walked over and glanced at the card. *Get*

THE FIANCÉ IS FINISHED

better soon. I'm here for you. Jack.

Interesting. I thought they were just friends, but perhaps the relationship had moved out of the friendship zone?

"I'm glad you're feeling better," Jack said as I returned to the living room. "We've got good news."

"What's that?"

"You can relax," I said. "The police have evidence that you aren't the killer. They should be leaving you alone from now on."

Darla's shoulders sagged as tears welled in her eyes. She glanced from me to Jack, and back again. "Are you sure?"

"Positive."

"How did you find out?"

"It's not important," he said. He obviously was serious about taking our promise of secrecy to the grave, with or without a blood pact. He sat down next to her and took her hand in his. "The important thing is that you don't have to worry about being a suspect any longer. You can concentrate on your business and your health."

As she rested her head on his shoulder, I

narrowed my gaze. They seemed quite chummy.

"Do you think these two are getting busy between the sheets?" Ruby asked, her thoughts mirroring mine. "At one time when she wasn't on her meds *she* thought they were dating, and Jack put the kibosh on that. But now... it looks like they may be."

When Jack placed his arm around her shoulders, I agreed one hundred percent. Between the flowers and the physical contact, it certainly appeared as if they'd taken the relationship in a different direction. I liked Jack, but I wasn't certain I approved of him dating Darla, especially in her fragile state of mind. He'd always been a womanizer and she didn't need his games in her life.

But then again, was their relationship really any of my business?

"So did Adam confirm I wasn't a suspect any longer?" Darla asked.

I nodded but didn't go into any details. I'd established she wasn't, but I'd done so through Adam's computer, so I'd give him the credit. Besides, I couldn't exactly be truthful on how the information had been obtained. Darla couldn't speak to Adam about it or mention my name. He'd realize I'd been up to something. "He's been really busy, so it's probably best not to discuss it with him."

"Well, I'd like to thank him." she said. "Maybe a quick text or something?"

"Not right now," Jack replied. "Let's just concentrate on getting the diner back open."

But Darla wouldn't let it go. "What was the evidence he gave you that proved I didn't kill that man?"

Jack and I exchanged glances, and I knew we'd have to give her more. "Well, there was security footage from the hotel. The killer had long black hair. That's definitely not you."

She reached for her blonde bun, fingering an escaped wisp. "No, it's not. But it could be you, Bernie."

I grabbed my ponytail and pulled it over my shoulder. After glancing at the split ends, I noted a haircut was in order. "You're right. If I wore my hair down, I could've definitely been in that video."

"So you saw it?" Darla asked. "He showed it to you?"

Ruby groaned and rolled her eyes. "So much for keeping a secret, Bernie. You don't need a blood pact. You need a muzzle."

"Um... no. He uh... he described what was on it to me."

Darla narrowed her gaze. "Why do I feel like I'm not getting the full story here?"

My cheeks heated as I avoided Jack's steely stare and glanced around the room.

"You're a terrible liar, Bernie," she said. "You always have been. Now I'm wondering if you're being dishonest with me and telling me all this so I won't have to think about it anymore. Are you lying to me for my own good or some nonsense like that?"

"No, she isn't," Jack said quickly. "I promise. She saw the video."

"Well, if Adam didn't show you, how did you view it?"

"The cat's out of the bag on this one," Ruby said. "I'd like to watch you try to bluff your way out, but I don't think that's going to happen."

Ruby was right. My mind was a blank

and I was a terrible liar. I wanted Darla to believe she was in the clear and to quit worrying about the murder investigation. The only way to do so was to tell her the truth.

"Darla, I asked Adam about the killing and he hasn't been helpful. Honestly, he didn't really have anything to give to me to prove your innocence. So I broke into his apartment and snooped around to find the evidence to clear you."

She gasped and turned to Jack. "Were you part of this?"

"No," I replied before he could answer. "He had nothing to do with it."

Jack gave me a slight nod and smile, appreciating my lies. If he had developed a romantic interest in Darla, he most likely didn't want her aware of his shady past—or his illegal activities of this afternoon.

"You did that... for me?" she asked.

I nodded. "But please... you can't ever say anything to Adam."

"Okay," she whispered. "I hope for your sake he never finds out."

"Me, too."

There were now two people—well, four,

if I counted Ruby and Ned—who knew of my indiscretion. The ghosts couldn't communicate with anyone, so I didn't have to worry about them. Ruby would never rat anyway, and I also had my doubts about Ned. With Jack's past, I didn't think he'd tell on me either. If he did, I could figuratively knife him in the back by sharing his involvement in the scheme. That left Darla. If Adam ever found out what I'd done, it would be because of her.

"So do you know who killed that man?" Darla asked. "Could you recognize a face in the video?"

I shook my head. "No, but based on the list of suspects that I'm aware of, it was his sister. She's the only one with long black hair."

"Why in the world would she kill her own brother?" Jack asked.

"Money," I replied.

Ruby spun around in a circle next to me. "Yep. You always have to follow the money."

"Seriously? She killed her brother over money?" Darla asked, furrowing her brow.

"Yes. The family was very wealthy. She'd

been cut out of the will when their parents died a few years ago. She's... she's had some issues in the past." I didn't have the energy to go into her drug problem and rehabilitation, and it wasn't really relevant to the conversation.

"So now she's got a bunch of cash and she'll be in prison," Darla said, shaking her head. "What a shame."

"At least she's got enough money for a good lawyer," Jack said. "Maybe he'll be able to get her a reduced sentence."

I nodded, suddenly sick to my stomach. The stress of the day had taken its toll. "I'm going to head out. I'll talk to you two later."

"Thank you, Bernie." Darla stood, then walked over and wrapped her arms around my neck. "What you did means so much to me."

"You're welcome."

As I closed the door behind me and Ruby, sprouts of self-hatred began to grow. I'd done a terrible thing and I couldn't seem to shake the guilt.

However, I'd have to learn to live with it,

especially if I wanted to keep seeing Adam, which I did.

My phone rang.

"Who is it?" Ruby asked. I pulled it out of my pocket and stared at it a moment trying to decipher who was on the other end. The sun shone directly on the screen making it impossible to see, so I took my chances and answered.

"Hey, Bernie," Adam said. "How are things going?"

Crud. "Fine, fine. How are you?"

"I'm tired, but everything's good here. I miss you."

"Same here," I said, sliding into my car while hoping I sounded normal and not the nervous wreck I felt like.

"I think we're going to wrap up this case pretty quickly," he said. "Do you want to get together?"

"Absolutely. I'd love to."

"Perfect. I'll give you a call in the next couple of days. Sounds good?"

"Yes. I'm looking forward to it. I can't wait to see you."

We said our goodbyes and I hung up.

Laying my head against the headrest, I closed my eyes for a moment as the icky feeling in my stomach intensified.

How in the world would I ever be able to meet Adam's gaze again without feeling as though I'd betrayed him?

CHAPTER 16

*A*fter a restless night's sleep, I staggered into the kitchen the next morning and put on a pot of coffee. There wouldn't be enough brew in the world to jerk me out of my foul mood, but I had to try.

As the liquid dripped into the canister, I pulled out a box of donuts from the pantry and set them out on the counter. When the coffee pot finished its job, I poured myself a large cup and flipped on the television. The local weatherman droned on about how—surprise!—the sun would be shining in Arizona for the rest of the week. I always imagined being a weather reporter in the state would be the most boring job. They could actually check in with the viewers every few months and no one would notice their absence because the weather was so darn predictable. Heck, I got excited when we had a few clouds pass by.

Amy and Cathy came downstairs and I tried to smile and wear my happy morning face, but I didn't succeed. The guilt of what I'd done pressed heavily on my soul, making it feel like I dragged a hundred-pound weight behind me.

"We came down for coffee," Amy said. I noticed she carried a black trash bag. "I'm just going to set this in the garbage. Is it out back?"

I nodded and pointed to the back door while trying to recall if I'd forgotten to empty the trashcans in her room when I'd emptied all the bins in the house yesterday. Brushing the question aside, I turned back to the coffee. A possible trash oversight? Who cared. Not me.

"Oh, wow!" Cathy declared as she shoved a donut into her mouth. "Turn it up!"

Ruby appeared behind her and stared at the television.

A video of Adam and Sheriff Walker walking out of the sheriff's department came up on the screen. I hurried over and jammed up the volume. Both of their faces were particularly grim, as if they didn't really like the cameras filming.

"Old Bruce has his serious face on," Ruby said. "He always looks like that when there's a television camera crew around."

A perky blonde newscaster appeared on the screen, smiling into the camera. "An arrest was made early this morning in the murder of Colin Victory, who was killed at the Sedona Grand Hotel earlier this week."

Footage played of Jessica being helped out of the sheriff's cruiser and into the building. Based on the atmospheric lighting, they'd arrested her just before dawn and I couldn't help but wonder where they'd roused her from. Her car? A park bench? Had she found a hotel room? Her long black hair hung down her cheeks acting as a curtain, just like it had done in the hotel security footage. I wished she'd push back the hair and give us a glimpse of her face. Was she crying? Angry she'd been caught?

Back to the newscaster. "Jessica Victory, the victim's sister, was apprehended without incident early this morning. She'll face murder charges."

The shot moved to her co-host, a man with salt and pepper hair and an overuse of teeth whitener. "From what we've been able to gather about her, this arrest shouldn't be a surprise. The perpetrator has a long, checkered history of past trouble."

So much for news. Why did every caster believe their audience wanted their opinions and diatribes? What happened to just reporting the facts?

"Really?" the blonde said, her eyes wide with surprise. "Do we have a motive as to why she allegedly killed her own brother?"

"Not yet, but we'll keep digging. As always, we're here reporting for you." He pointed at the camera and smiled broadly. I waited for him to give us all a wink. "Serving you the news that you want to hear. Let's toss it over to Bob, who's sharing the live traffic report this morning from the highway!"

"Oh, my gosh," Amy said, bringing her hand to her heart. "It's over."

I turned down the volume as poor Bob stood on the side of the road and began his spiel. While he talked, cars and trucks whizzed by. Hopefully, he'd remain safe. Frankly, no one should be standing on the side of the freeway unless absolutely necessary, and I didn't understand how Bob taking his life into his own hands improved the newscast.

"It is," Cathy agreed. "What a relief."

Ruby shook her head. "I don't know, Bernie. Something doesn't seem right to me. It's all too neat and tidy."

Cathy's brow furrowed as she glanced over at me. "Bernie, I have to ask... and I do this without judgment. But are you smoking weed? Every now and then I catch a little whiff of it. Last night was particularly bad. It was like someone was lying next to me in bed puffing away."

I glanced over her shoulder at Ruby, who shrugged. "What can I say?" she said. "I was bored. Yes, I crawled into bed with her and yelled at her for a few minutes to see if she'd notice me. She didn't."

"No, I don't smoke pot." Grinding my jaw, I turned away from them and marched over to the coffee pot to fetch another cup. I didn't care who my grandmother haunted. My irritation wasn't with her, but with the case. I felt no respite at Jessica's arrest. In fact, it only worsened my mood. Yes, I'd seen a woman with long black hair in that video. It was irrefutable evidence. But Ruby was right. Something seemed off and I couldn't put my finger on it either.

Cathy moved to comfort Amy when she burst into tears again. I stared at them both while sipping my coffee. I had no reason to be upset with either one, yet I wanted them out of my sight. It took a moment to realize, but what I really wanted was to separate myself... from myself. Amy and Cathy had done nothing wrong. I was furious and disgusted with me.

"I've got to get ready for class," I muttered, striding into my bedroom before they could answer. After setting my coffee cup on the dresser, I took a few deep breaths and attempted to relax. I found Elvira on the windowsill soaking up the morning sun. As I tried to pet her, she hissed and took a swipe at me. At the moment, even my cat didn't like me.

"You better take a chill pill, Bernie," Ruby said after ghosting through the door.

"I know," I whispered, when I really wanted to scream. However, I couldn't chance Cathy and Amy overhearing me in the kitchen. "I'm in the middle of a good session of self-hatred for what I did."

"You had to help Darla." Ruby lay across the bed. Elvira joined her and glared at me as I reached out to pet her. My attempt at loving my feline was again met with a hiss. "She doesn't like it when you're all stressed out. You give off bad juju."

I whispered a curse as my cat snuggled the ghost and began to purr.

"Don't beat yourself up over it," Ruby said. "Our plan went flawlessly. He'll never find out what you did. There weren't any witnesses."

"Darla knows," I said as I pulled on my

socks and sneakers. "If he finds out, it's because of her. I don't think Jack will say anything."

"Mr. Dimples is a hardened criminal. He's aware of the code. He'll follow it."

I stared at my grandmother for a moment and shook my head. Listening to her talk about criminal codes of conduct almost made me laugh. If my mood wasn't so foul, I would have. Sure, she'd been arrested a number of times, but there was a significant difference between being put in jail for drunken public nudity versus burglary.

"Where are we headed off to?" Ruby asked.

"I've got class with Jezebel."

"Are you going to kick some butt and take names?"

I sighed and grabbed my sunglasses. "I hope so, Ruby. I really hope so." Because I felt like I was failing in every other facet of my life.

WHEN I ENTERED THE BAR, I was on the lookout for Jezebel. She wouldn't catch me with one of her surprise attacks again.

"Hey, Bernie!" she said, coming out from the back room. "Good to see you, girl. Did you see that they caught the bad guy? Or in this case, the bad girl?"

"Yes, I did."

"Never underestimate a woman. I don't know when men are going to learn that. Is Ruby here?" I nodded. Like my ghost would ever allow me to step foot in Tip 'Em Back without her. "Ruby!" Jezebel yelled. "You smell like hot dog water!"

Ruby rolled her eyes and crossed her arms over her chest. "I'm an acquired taste, Jezebel. If you don't like me, simply acquire some taste."

I threw my head back and laughed until tears streamed down my face. And it felt fantastic as the stress flowed from my body. Maybe Ruby was right. Perhaps laughter was the best medicine.

"She totally burned me, didn't she?" Jezebel asked, her eyes glittering with mischief.

"Oh, yeah." I repeated the insult.

"Wow. She won," Jezebel said, also breaking out into laughter. "Let's get to work. How're you feeling today?"

Miserable. Guilty. Worried. Stressed. "I'm fine."

She narrowed her gaze on me. "I don't believe you, but whatever."

"I did something I shouldn't have," I blurted, surprised. I'd had no intention of sharing my problems with Jezebel when I'd first entered the bar, but the words tumbled out. "I'm feeling horrible about it."

Jezebel stared at me a long moment and tucked a lock of blonde hair behind her ear. "Did you make a choice to do this something?"

"I didn't really feel I had a choice. I had to... I had to help someone."

"You always have a choice, Bernie. Always. You didn't need to help anyone. You could have been a complete jerk and turned your back on that person, but you didn't."

"I broke another person's trust... if they find out what I did."

"Then make sure they don't," Jezebel

said, shrugging. "We all have our secrets... our ghosts in the closet. Except you lead yours around like a dog on a leash." Jezebel cackled at her own joke. "We're even, old woman!"

Ruby shook her head and I was surprised she lacked a snappy comeback. My ghost seemed to be losing her touch.

"Let's go work out," Jezebel said. "It always makes me feel better to imagine beating the stuffing out of someone."

I followed her into the back room where she'd laid out the mats. I caught the jump rope she threw at me and began the workout.

By the time we got to the squats, an energy had built up within me—anger, guilt, and sadness being the main drivers. When Jezebel and I finished the warmup and we squared off, sweat poured down my brow and my breath came in deep, heavy pulls. My mind focused as I zeroed in on her, watching her every move.

She came at me from the front, and I side-stepped out of the way, then jammed my elbow down into her back without restraint. She hissed and rubbed the area, while I relished in the feeling of triumph. I wasn't even worried about hurting her as I had been in the past.

Jezebel quickly attacked me again. This time, she maneuvered behind me and got her arm around my neck. I leaned forward and elbowed her in the ribs, then flipped her over my shoulder and onto the mats. The shift in weight caused me to lose my balance and I almost fell on top of her, but I caught myself at the last second. As I hovered over her, she stared up at me, her eyes wide in shock.

No one was more surprised than me. I brought my hand up to my mouth and stepped away from the toughest, most formidable woman I'd ever met.

As she grinned, I said, "Jezebel, I am so sorry. I—"

"Stop right there," she said, standing. "You acted on instinct and it was perfect. I was wondering if we'd ever get to this place, and I'm so happy to finally see you tossing me around."

She took me into a big bear hug and

squeezed. For a second, I considered it a sneak attack, but I realized it was a show of friendship, of respect. I relaxed into the hug and allowed the accolades to warm me.

"I didn't know if you had it in you, Bernie," she said. "You're going to be one heck of a butt-kicker, my friend."

As she released me, pride welled within. Those words coming from her meant something.

"Pretty soon, you'll be able to kill a man with your bare hands," she said with a chuckle. "Knife a guy before he even sees it coming." She gave me a wink. "Not that I'd really know anything about that."

CHAPTER 17

*A*s I drove home from Tip 'Em Back, Jezebel's words played over and over in my mind. Had she been joking, or had she just admitted to killing a man?

"I can practically hear your thoughts!" Ruby said. "Jezzy didn't kill anyone!"

"Then why did she say that I'd be able to knife a man without him seeing me coming?"

"Because she's Jezzy! That's what she does! She says stuff to shock people!"

I shook my head. "Maybe it was her way of admitting to the crime."

"Bernie, if Jezebel was going to kill someone, she'd never cop to it. She'd keep herself so far off the radar, she'd be invisible to investigators."

"I'm sure you're right," I muttered.

"And she's got blonde hair. That person who did the killing had black hair. You saw for yourself."

Of course. That little fact was the clincher. I was reading too much into Jezebel's statement.

"They've got the killer in custody," Ruby said. "Darla seemed better. All is right in this world of yours. Can you relax for a while? Please?! You're going to be dead by the time you hit forty if you don't stop all this worry and stress!"

When I stopped at the light, I turned to my ghost. "You said you thought something was wrong with the story when they showed the arrest on the television."

"I'm aware," Ruby replied. "But I was probably mistaken."

With a gasp, I placed my hand over my mouth in mock surprise. "I thought that never happened!"

"It doesn't." She chuckled, the laugh lines around her eyes stretching to her hairline.

"Mark it on the calendar. A national day of importance. The day Ruby the ghost was wrong! To celebrate, tequila shots for everyone!"

A horn honked behind me and I glanced up to find the light had turned green. Ruby muttered something about patience being a virtue and then cursed the driver.

With a sigh, I sped up and drove home.

After parking in the dirt lot behind my home, I walked inside and immediately knew the house was empty. Somehow I'd developed the ability to decipher whether my guests were around or not. It sounded strange, but the air felt different. And the fact Elvira had stretched out on the living room sofa was also a good indicator as she really didn't like anyone except Ruby. In fact, she didn't care for living people in general.

I settled in next to the cat and Ruby took a seat on the couch across from me. Elvira jumped from the cushions and curled up next to her. If my ghost ever went to her final resting place, the cat would be devastated and probably go search for another haunted home.

"So what are we doing the rest of the day?" Ruby asked.

I shrugged and rubbed my shoulder. I was perpetually sore from my workouts and felt like I could sleep for weeks. "First, I need to shower. I worked up a big sweat at Jezebel's. After that, I don't have any plans. I'm waiting for Adam to call. What do you want to do?"

"Well, I was thinking—"

The doorbell rang.

With a groan, I stood to answer.

"Tell whoever it is to go away!" Ruby yelled. "I'm sick of company!"

Never thought I'd hear her say that. She usually loved visitors.

As I strode to the door, I glanced at my phone for notification of a reservation. Nothing. I opened it to find Adam grinning at me and carrying his laptop—the scene of my crime.

"I wasn't expecting you!" I said, my stomach curling and heat traveling from my neck to my cheeks. Quickly leaning my head against his chest, I wrapped my arms around his waist to hide my blush. He held me close.

"Do you have time for me today?" he asked, kissing the top of my head.

"Of course! I always have time for you. Come in."

We walked arm-in-arm into the living room and sat down together on the couch. I glanced over at Ruby, hoping to convey I'd like some time alone with Adam.

"Hey, copper!" she greeted.

I relayed the message and pointed in her direction.

Adam smiled and waved. "Hi, Ruby. I was wondering if I could have a little alone time with my girlfriend?"

"Aww... isn't that sweet. Sure. I'll just be hanging around doing the ghostly things I do." She faded from view, her body rippling slowly until nothing remained except an angry cat. Elvira meowed loudly and stalked from the room.

"I saw you on television," I said.

Adam chuckled. "How did I look?"

"Serious and all business." I giggled. "I'm so glad the case is over."

Adam set down his computer on the coffee table. "Me too. It was a tough one. I don't think we could have solved it without the video from the hotel. Thank goodness for technology."

"I'm glad they were able to give it to you. W-what was on it?"

While trying to act like I hadn't seen the footage before him, I hesitated before speaking, which caused the conversation to become very jilted.

"Strangely enough, all the suspects were blonde, except one."

"Colin's sister?"

"Yes. How did you know?"

"She was here." I glanced around the living room trying to decide what I should tell, if any of it. My story could lead to more questions and take me down a path with Adam I didn't want to go. "She was looking for a place to stay but decided to go somewhere else. And of course, I saw her on television."

One thing though had bothered me from

the beginning. "How did she know where her brother was? He lived in Phoenix, and no one seems to have a clue where Jessica resided. They weren't very close. How did she find out Colin was in town?"

"Colin and Jessica were working on their relationship. She actually lives in Prescott, and when Colin came up here to win back Amy, he called her and asked if they could meet. She said she'd come to him."

Prescott was about an hour and a half drive from Sedona.

I furrowed my brow. "She said she came because she received word her brother had been murdered. Not to visit him."

"That's true. Once we identified him, we called her. The plan had been for her to meet with him after he smoothed things over with Amy."

"And instead, she arrived early and murdered him?"

"Yes. And became very wealthy for her troubles."

I wanted to move past this murder and into our future together, so I tried to change the subject. "Should we have a date night tonight? Maybe dinner and a movie? I'm not sure what's out, but we can look."

"How's Darla?" Adam asked. "Is she feeling better now that the killer has been caught?" He apparently wasn't quite ready to put the ugly incident behind us.

"I haven't talked to her today, but I saw her yesterday. She was good. Definitely getting better."

"The diner was closed last time I drove by."

"Yes. Between the investigation and running her business, she realized she couldn't do it all. So she closed, but I understand she's working with Jack to open back up."

"That's good news."

"I think they may be dating, but I haven't confirmed that."

"Interesting. I wasn't aware Jack liked her any more than as a friend."

"Yes. What about that dinner and movie now?"

Adam stared at me for a long moment, then smiled. "I wanted to show you something."

"What's that?" I asked.

He grabbed his laptop and opened it. After a few clicks, he pulled up the grainy hotel footage I'd already seen but couldn't admit to it.

"What am I looking at?" I asked, hoping I sounded sincere.

"This is the hotel footage."

"Oh, wow! Are you going to play it?"

He nodded and we watched Jessica walk down the hallway and into the room, then a few minutes later, flee the scene of the crime with blood on her sweatshirt.

"That's incredible," I said, trying to convince Adam I was surprised and shocked.

"Yes. She was caught red-handed."

"It's hard to imagine she didn't take the cameras into account. I mean, she does attempt to hide her face, but it seems like she would try to avoid being seen at all."

We sat in silence for a moment as I stared at the computer screen and Adam's gaze bore into me.

Did he believe my act?

"I have one other thing to show you. Do you want to see it?"

"Sure," I replied as I linked my arm through his and laid my head on his shoulder, snuggling in closer. "Is it the movie schedule for tonight?"

"No. It's definitely interesting though."

He clicked a couple of buttons and another video appeared. I immediately recognized it as the inside of his condo. I stifled a gasp.

There wasn't any sound on the recording. I probably wouldn't have heard it anyway with how hard my heart thumped in my chest.

Adam came into the frame from the hallway and grabbed his keys off the kitchen counter, right where the camera had been set up. He walked off screen toward the front door.

Moments later, I entered the frame. A cold sweat overcame me as I watched myself hurry into the living room, sit down, study a few papers, then grab his laptop.

Tears sprang to my eyes while Adam sat stone-still. Why in the world had he put a camera in his condo?

"Remember how I told you Ned thought

he was being funny by hiding my stuff?" Adam asked, his voice low, obviously somehow reading my mind.

I nodded, unable to speak.

"I was wasting so much time searching for my things, so I installed a camera to be able to see where he hid my stuff. I thought I had him beat at his own game. A centuries old ghost wouldn't understand a camera. Imagine my surprise when I was looking at past footage to find where he hid my shoe and I ran across this."

Wiping my cheeks, I sat up and unlaced my arm from his.

"This is the best part," he said, pointing at the screen where I rose from the couch and stood in the middle of the room. My mouth and hands moved, as if I were speaking, which I had been. Ned and Ruby had been standing right in front of me. "You're talking to the ghosts there, aren't you?"

I nodded.

"So not only did you break into my apartment, look at my computer and papers, you cajoled my ghost into cooperating?"

"He didn't like me being there without you," I whispered, crossing my arms over my chest. I couldn't meet Adam's gaze.

"I think I know the answer, but what were you looking for, Bernie?"

My tears flowed freely now. Dang it! My worst fears had come true.

"You saw the video footage from the hotel, didn't you?" he asked. On the computer, I returned to the couch and poked through his laptop once again, then set it down and stood. I quickly turned back to it.

"The camera time matches the time the email came in, so there's no need to lie. I know you saw it."

"I had to help Darla," I whispered, wiping my nose on my sweatshirt.

"How did you get in?" Adam asked. "The lock wasn't jimmied. Did Ned open the door for you?"

I shook my head. I'd never give up Jack. "Ned had nothing to do with it. How I entered doesn't matter."

Adam shut the laptop and sighed. "You broke into my house, looked at classified papers and at my computer, and then pretended nothing happened?"

"I'm sorry, Adam. Darla was going to have a breakdown because she couldn't stop thinking about being a suspect. Her paranoia was off the charts. She's come so far and I didn't want her to slide backward."

"I specifically told you that we would get the killer and I couldn't give you any information on the case."

"Yes, you did."

"And you broke the law. Not to mention my trust."

I rubbed my forehead, still unable to meet his gaze. "I'm so sorry, Adam."

"So am I, Bernie." He stood. "I need to go." He strode toward the front door.

"Adam, wait!"

"No, Bernie," he said, turning around, his face contorted in anger. "There's nothing to wait for. You and I... we're done."

CHAPTER 18

"Did you cry this much when I died?" Ruby asked. She'd perched herself on the edge of my bathtub and stared down at me with a furrowed brow. Elvira also studied me with hooded lids from the doorway, her tail swishing back and forth. Vanilla and lavender bubble surrounded me and a half-empty bottle of wine sat on the floor. My tears came endlessly.

"Yes," I whispered, which was the truth. Even though I'd lost touch with Ruby in her last years, when I discovered she'd died, it had devastated me. A part of my past had been taken away... a really, really good part. With Adam walking out on me, it was another loss, but one of the present and the future. Adam and I had been almost perfect together and I realized I had fallen in love with him, though I'd never told him so. The pain of not having him in my life cut deep.

"Well, I'm flattered, but all these tears aren't going to bring him back. Men aren't worth crying over, Bernie."

"Adam was," I sniffed, taking another sip of wine.

Ruby sighed and shook her head. "Are you going soak until you're pruned-up and run out of hot water? You've been in there for over an hour."

Speaking of which... using my toe, I turned on the hot water spigot and warmed the water once again.

"This self-pity isn't a flattering look on you, Bernie."

I didn't care what Ruby thought. My past wasn't exactly littered with romantic inter-ludes and I'd lost the one man who had held my interest. And I'd been the cause of it. My own stupid actions.

"Never should have done it," I muttered.

"Yes, you should have. You made the

right decision. Who knows where Darla would be right now if you hadn't stepped in and helped her? Probably a psychiatric ward. Or what if she'd committed suicide? Or tried to blow up the sheriff's office like she'd threatened? What then, Bernie? Your friend was in a very fragile state of mind. Even though you broke the law and Adam's trust, you did the right thing."

"It doesn't feel that way."

"Of course it doesn't. A lot of times, that's the way it is when you're backed up against a wall and cornered like a feral cat. Do you do the right thing and potentially screw everything up, or do nothing at all and watch Darla implode? Oftentimes, the right choice isn't always the easiest."

Staring at my ghost, I tried to imagine how I'd feel if Darla had been hospitalized again, or in jail for trying to detonate the sheriff's department. Or worse, if she'd committed suicide. I would be kicking myself for not helping her.

"I can't believe he installed a camera," I muttered.

Ruby shook her head. "Me, neither. I

told Ned it would be funny to hide Adam's stuff every now and then, but it sounded like he took the game to a whole other level if a camera was needed to find things."

I was so upset, I couldn't even be angry at Ruby for giving Ned such horrible ideas. I had no energy for it. "Why do you think he can move things when you can't?" I asked.

"Bernie, I have no idea. Why are Ned and I trapped here? Maybe he can play his silly game because he's been dead longer than me? Perhaps ghosts become more formidable the longer we're stuck here?"

If true, that was bad news for me. I liked Ruby being helpless and harmless. If she became powerful and could cause other-worldly happenings such as send books flying through the air or hide my shoes, it wouldn't bode well for me in the least bit. Her love of mischief could make my life miserable.

"I usually don't recommend something like this, but you need to put that bottle of wine away," she said, standing. "Get out of this tub. You've got things to do."

"Like what?"

"Don't Cathy and Amy want sunset yoga or something?"

I wasn't in any condition to teach it. "Class has been canceled," I murmured.

"Do they know that?"

"They will when I don't show up."

Ruby sighed and swore under her breath. "This isn't like you, Bernie. That's very *irresponsible*. You are anything but that. Now get out of the tub. The pity party is over."

"No."

She placed her hands on her hips and glared at me. "You are in your mid-thirties, not a toddler. Quit acting like one. No man is worth this." Elvira followed when she strode off into my bedroom.

I shut my eyes and tried to forget about my broken heart. My efforts only brought more tears. Maybe Ruby was right. Sitting in the tub wallowing in my sadness and wine wasn't going to do me any favors and perhaps, it was only making things worse.

Taking a deep breath, I stood on wobbly legs and stepped out of the tub. After wrapping a towel around my torso, I stared at my reflection. Puffy face, tired eyes, red nose. Attractive.

"Someone's knocking at the door!" Ruby yelled. "Go answer it!"

"I'd like to put some clothes on first," I replied.

"Why? What if it's some cute delivery driver willing to take your mind off Adam? Without clothes, you've won half the battle!"

I hurried into the bedroom not bothering to answer and slipped on my sweats and sweatshirt. A chill hung in the air, causing me to shiver—winter was just around the corner, which meant the holidays. My original plan had been to share them with Adam and invite my parents for Christmas, but they'd already declined. Adam had dumped me. That meant I'd be spending them alone with my dead grandmother. "Oh, my word," I whispered. "Can things get much worse?"

I strode out of my bedroom and heard Amy and Cathy talking upstairs. Although I appreciated the money, I wished they'd leave. I wanted to be alone.

Opening the door, I found Jack. He smiled.

"Mr. Dimples!" Ruby squealed. "He's the perfect one to take your mind off Adam! You should've answered the door naked!"

A slow blush crawled over my cheeks. This was one of those times I was so thankful no one but me could hear my ghost. "Hi, Jack."

"You're looking a little rough," he said, crossing his arms and leaning against the doorframe.

"Thanks. I feel a little rough. Glad everything is matching up. Come on in."

I led him to the kitchen and pointed at the stool. "I'll be right back." After retrieving my bottle from the bathroom, I asked if he wanted any, but noted he'd helped himself to a glass of water.

"No, thanks," he replied, holding up his cup. "This is fine with me right now."

Good. More for me. "What's up?"

"Adam came by."

I poured more wine and fought back tears. "That's nice."

"He told me you two broke up."

"Yes. He dumped me just as he should have."

Jack sighed and shook his head. "He's pretty upset, Bernie, but he'll come around."

"No, he won't," I replied. "I broke his trust. It's over. How much did he tell you?"

"Everything," he said. "He even told me about the video of you in his condo."

But Adam hadn't *shown* him. He wouldn't be able to explain me speaking and gesturing to apparently nothing. He wanted to keep the ghosts a secret. "I never would've gone in if I had known about the camera."

"Yeah, that was one strike of bad luck. He said it was new, and he wondered how many other times you'd been inside his house without him knowing."

"Never," I replied. "Even if I wanted to, I had no way of getting in."

"He's still trying to figure how you managed that, which leads me to believe you didn't mention me."

"Of course not. I said I wouldn't."

"Well, I appreciate it."

"Rats get shanked," Ruby said from behind Jack. "The code is alive and well in this house, buddy."

I took a long sip of wine as I stared at Mr. Dimples over the rim and wondered what was going on between him and Darla.

"How is she?" I asked, knowing full well he was aware who I spoke of.

"Better, because of what you did. We're opening the diner in a couple days after she restocks."

I nodded and set down my glass. If I were such a big hero, why did I feel like such a big zero? "What's the deal with you two?"

Jack shrugged and grinned. "I really don't know. When she went off her meds and you shared she thought we were dating, I was a little freaked out by it. I don't like to be tied down."

With a snort, I rolled my eyes. "That's putting it nicely."

Ignoring my jab, he continued. "But after she was hospitalized and she came home, I started to spend a lot of time with her. Just checking up on her, running errands... stuff like that. And... well, I like her. I like being with her."

Was Sedona's womanizer ready to settle down? Perhaps, but I needed to be certain my friend was safe and Jack held no ill intentions. "Darla's state of mind is fragile, Jack. I hope you won't do anything to hurt her. If you like her, fine. If you want a relationship, great. But don't hurt her, okay?"

"It's different with her," Jack said. "I don't know what it is... I can't put my finger on it. But I... I just don't want to be with anyone else."

Unable to believe his words, I simply stared. The town stallion had been tamed? What was next? Unicorn sightings?

"I like being needed," he added, shrugging. "I like taking care of her and doing things for her."

More tears sprang to my eyes as my heart melted into a pile of goo and my self-pity returned with such force, my chest ached. "I'm happy for you two," I whispered, and moved my gaze to the counter.

"I'm sorry. I shouldn't be talking like that with you being so upset. I really came over here to tell you that I think Adam is angry right now, but he'll get over it."

I nodded with pursed lips, having zero faith that Jack spoke the truth. Adam's last words had been so final. *We're done.* Not, *I'm mad and I need space, but I'll call you in a few days.*

"I also wanted to thank you for not mentioning me to Adam," Jack said, standing. "It's appreciated, and I owe you big time."

After taking a deep breath, I walked him to the door where he gave me a quick hug. When I shut the panel, I stood staring at it for a long time, unable to move. I heard the cars driving down the street, Amy and Cathy chatting upstairs, the birds chirping in the trees. My life had come to a complete standstill. My heart shattered into a thousand pieces while I seemed to be frozen in the perpetual state of heartache and loss. Yet, everything around me continued to go on as if my life hadn't been turned upside down. A strange dichotomy, indeed.

"Come on, Bernie," Ruby said, appearing next to me. "Get it together, girl. You're starting to scare me."

I smiled at my ghost, wiped the tears tracking down my cheeks, and returned to my bedroom. Closing the blinds, I turned off the lights and locked the door. After curling up under the covers, I placed a pillow over my head and shut my eyes, willing my sorrow to leave.

Maybe tomorrow I would be able to pull my life together, but not today.

CHAPTER 19

A fitful sleep brought the morning sun and with it came a bit of a headache. After popping a couple ibuprofen, I went for a run to clear my fuzzy brain and the rest of the wine from my system. By the time I'd completed three miles, my mood had improved slightly. It got even better when I arrived home to find Cathy and Amy in the kitchen and they shared they'd be leaving in the afternoon.

"It's been a horrible stay, but you've been a fabulous host," Amy said while hugging me. "We really appreciate your hospitality."

"I'm sorry about Colin," I replied, stepping away from her. "I hope you can find some peace."

"She will," Cathy said. "Thanks for everything, Bernie."

I retreated to my room where I showered, changed the sheets and straightened up a bit. Then, I tackled the kitchen. One nice thing about Amy and Cathy was they were very neat and tidy, which made them easy guests to have around. Less work was always appreciated.

After a quick cleanout of the fridge, I pulled the garbage bag from the canister and hurried for the back door. As I stepped outside, a chill ran down my spine. With my wet hair and the cool, fall air, I became cold quickly.

Just as I was about to dump the bag into the trash can, I saw the one Amy had brought out a couple of days ago. Going through the garbage grossed me out, but I should make sure there wasn't anything that should be recycled. Besides, the bag had originated from her bedroom. Probably water bottles and tissues—no rotting food or anything.

I pulled it out and opened it up. With a gasp, I dropped it, stepped away and brought my hand to my mouth. Had that been... a human head?

No. Of course not. I was seeing things. My lack of sleep, and the hangover was causing me to hallucinate. After approaching the trash again, I reached in and pulled out the bag, slowly opening it. Dipping shaky fingers inside, I pulled out strands of black hair. Thankfully, not a head, but a wig. A whiff of a coppery stench wafted from the bag. I dropped the wig and turned the plastic inside out. A bloodied gray sweatshirt fell to the ground.

"Oh my goodness," I gasped as I stared at my find.

Flashbacks of the hotel surveillance video came to me—a woman with long black hair wearing a gray hoodie. When she ran from the scene, it had blood all over the front... just like the one at my feet.

Why would Jessica need a wig? She wouldn't. But someone trying disguise themselves? Heck yes.

I quickly picked up the evidence and

shoved it back into the trash bag, glancing around to make sure no one was watching me. Taking a few deep breaths, I hurried toward the back door. I had to preserve the evidence, call Sheriff Walker and tell him he had arrested the wrong person. The murderer wasn't in jail, but in my dang house!

Once inside, I beelined for my bedroom where I found Ruby and Elvira lying on the bed together.

"What's in the bag?" Ruby asked as I stood in the middle of the room and frantically searched for a place to hide it. Dresser? Under the bed? Finally, I decided on my closet. I pulled out the dirty clothes hamper and jammed the bag into the corner, then replaced the brimming basket.

I turned to my ghost. "Where's my phone?"

Ruby shrugged. "Haven't paid much attention to where you put it last."

Glancing around my bedroom, I didn't find the device on any of the usual surfaces. Where had I placed it last night? The kitchen? I rushed in and searched the countertops. Nothing. Then I patted myself down, feeling my sweatshirt and jeans. It wouldn't be the first time I looked for my phone only to discover it in my pocket.

I tried to retrace my steps, but unfortunately, the evening was hazy at best. After the bath, Jack had come over. Then I'd gone to bed, but I'd been up a few times during the night. I didn't recall speaking to anyone. Maybe the phone had fallen under my bed?

Back in the bedroom, I dropped to my knees and pulled up the bedspread. Nothing.

"What the heck is going on?" Ruby asked. "You're running around here like you've got bugs in your panties."

Leaning toward her, I whispered, "I found a bloody sweatshirt and a long black wig in the garbage outside."

Her eyes widened and she sat up. "Like what the killer was wearing?"

"Yes. Amy took out the trash the other day. I was going to see if there was anything for recycling in there, but I found the murder disguise instead. Now I can't find my dang phone to call the police!"

"I'll help you look," she said, springing to

her feet. "We have to play it cool though. We can't let Amy know we're on to her and her evil ways."

Ruby ghosted out of the room while I kept searching in the bedroom. Nothing in the nightstands. Or the dresser. Perhaps I'd slipped it into a drawer in the kitchen in my wine-induced haze?

I ran out to the kitchen to find Cathy. "What's going on?" she asked. "Did you lose something? I heard you rummaging around and opening and shutting drawers."

"Y-yes," I said. "My phone. I've misplaced it."

"That's too bad. Can I help you look?"

"No. It's fine. I'll handle it. You don't need to bother."

Cathy furrowed her brow. "Are you okay? Where were you last night for yoga?"

"Yeah... I'm sorry about that," I said, crossing my arms over my chest. "My boyfriend dumped me yesterday afternoon and I was pretty upset. I wasn't in any condition for yoga."

Cathy shook her head. "Men. They're all jerks."

Actually, *I* had been the jerk, although I didn't see a reason to correct her. But, back to the fact I had a murderer in my house who was about to leave town and I couldn't find my phone to alert the police. I slid open a few drawers and didn't see the device. Where had I put it?!

"So are you going to kill him?" Cathy asked.

I froze, then slowly turned around. Maybe Amy wasn't the killer. Had Cathy committed murder?

"I'm just kidding," Cathy said, smiling. "Very inappropriate joke. We're going to be taking off as soon as Amy's ready."

Really inappropriate. "It's been lovely having you two here again," I replied, hoping I sounded sincere. My weight shifted from foot to foot and I couldn't re-main still. I *did* feel like I had bugs in my panties as Ruby had alluded to earlier.

My ghost appeared behind Cathy and rolled her eyes. "Lovely having these two psychopaths here if you like serial killer movies. Otherwise, it's creepier than a cemetery at night."

I couldn't argue.

"Just let them go, Bernie," Ruby continued. "Get them out of here."

I nodded. Ruby was right. In fact, I should just locate my keys, crawl into my SUV and head directly to the Sheriff's Department.

"Are you okay?" Cathy asked, laying her hand on my shoulder.

"Fine," I replied, flinching at her touch. I tried to cover up my uneasiness with a smile. "I'm going to keep searching for my phone."

In reality, my focus had shifted to my keys. I was worse at keeping track of those than my phone.

When she continued to stare at me, I grinned again and quickly walked through the downstairs one last time yet not finding either my keys or my phone. I returned to the bedroom and shut the door.

Leaning up against the panel, I shut my eyes.

"Found the phone!" Ruby yelled from the bathroom. "It's on top of the toilet!"

Of course. Where else would it be?

Everyone should keep their cell phones on top of the dang toilet. I must have set it there after my bath.

I rushed into the bathroom, sat down on the edge of the tub, and quickly looked up the non-emergency number for the Sheriff's Department, noting Jezebel had called numerous times and even left a few messages. I didn't have time to phone her back—more important pressing matters.

Sure, I could call 9-1-1, but was my life in danger? No. The killer didn't know I was aware of her. Besides, 9-1-1 meant lights and sirens. If she heard them coming, she could run or even hurt me if she felt trapped. I needed to explain to the sheriff or one of his deputies what I had found and tell them to approach my house quietly and cautiously.

"Please don't answer, please don't answer," I whispered as the phone rang. Meaning Adam, of course. I wanted to speak to anyone but him. Resting my forehead on my hand and my elbow on my knee, my damp hair fell around my face and suddenly, I felt very warm. Stress: the internal roasting mechanism.

"Sheriff's office. Deputy Gallagher." I almost hung up and tried again. Almost. Regardless of how badly I didn't want to speak to him, more important things were at stake than my hurt feelings and his anger.

"It's Bernie," I whispered. "I need you to listen very carefully to me."

Adam sighed. "I'm at work. This isn't the time or place to discuss our relationship. I told you: it's over."

"I don't want to talk about us," I hissed. Well, actually I did. I wanted to beg for forgiveness and plead for us to get back together. But as he mentioned, not the time or place. "I found a black wig and a bloody sweatshirt in my trashcan, Adam. You have the wrong person in custody."

The line went eerily quiet, and I wondered if he had hung up.

"Is this some type of trick to get me to come over there?"

I held the phone away from my face and stared at it a long moment. Seriously? He thought that little of me? "No. I would never do something like that."

"It's impossible for me to trust anything you say anymore, Bernie."

Clenching my fist in irritation, I stood and began to pace the bathroom tiles. "That's fine. Put someone on the phone who is willing to help me, Adam. The Sheriff's Department has a serious issue on their hands and you bringing your personal life into this isn't doing anyone any good."

"Don't tell me how to do my job," he said, his tone low and angry.

"I'm simply asking you to perform your job to the best of your ability and either help me or put someone on the phone who will!"

Ruby appeared in front of me and shook her head, then placed her finger over her lips. "Put a sock in it, girl. You're loud enough to summon a deaf demon."

Elevator music began to play over the line and tears sprung to my eyes. I was calling for help and he'd put me on hold. Had I truly broken things that significantly?

"Sheriff's office," a woman said.

I explained my situation once again. "Someone needs to come over here and get this evidence and arrest the right person!"

"Is this some type of prank?"

"No! I swear to you it isn't! Please just send someone over!" After giving my address, she promised me a deputy would be at my place within the hour.

I took a few deep breaths and tried to not think about Adam. Then I strode out into the kitchen for a glass of water.

As I stood at the sink and drained the glass, the back door opened and Amy marched in. As soon as she saw me, her pretty face somehow morphed into something evil. She placed her hands on her hips and glared at me. "Where is it, Bernie?"

The fact that she'd just come from where the trashcans were kept indicated she'd been looking for the evidence. I had to buy some time until the cops arrived. After setting my glass down, I took a few steps back. "Where's what?"

CHAPTER 20

For every step I took away from her, she came toward me. "I was just out to the garbage can. It's not there, Bernie. You found it. Where did you put it?"

I stepped to my right to angle the kitchen island between us. "I don't know what you're talking about."

"There are other bags in the cans, so I know the truck didn't come." She placed her hands on her hips and glared at me. "Where's the trash bag?"

"Don't tell her, Bernie!" Ruby yelled, appearing right next to Amy. "You keep your focus on me, not this crazy snot rag."

"I can't believe you killed him," I said,

shaking my head. "I can understand being upset, but to knife someone because he cheated on you? That's cold, Amy. How did you know about Jessica?"

"She's been sniffing around for over a year via email and texts I saw while going through Colin's phone. I realized she was trying to get back into his good graces and get her grubby mitts on the family money that should be mine."

What?! "It's their family money but you think it should belong to you?"

"Oh, this one is something else," Ruby said, shaking her head. "I knew she was guilty."

Amy's face contorted in anger as she pursed her lips. "I've put up with him all these years!" she shouted. "All the infidelity! Of course it should be mine!"

As I backstepped out of the kitchen into the dining room, I was almost ready to make a break for the front door and get the heck out of the house and away from the psychopath. But curiosity got the best of me. "How were you going to get the money if Colin was dead?"

She smiled at me and I realized she couldn't wait to reveal her scheme. "We were weeks away from marriage. I convinced him to have a will drawn up naming me, his wife, as the sole heir. He didn't want to do it at first, especially since we weren't married. We compromised. The will was made to my specifications, but we agreed to wait to sign it until after our wedding day. I have the will. A signature is easy to forge. I present it with a lot of flair and tears, and the money's mine."

"Jessica will fight you on it."

"Jessica's in prison for murder, which is where she's going to stay."

"She can still fight you," I said.

"Yes, she can, but who is the court going to believe? The bereaved fiancée, or the drug addicted sister who hasn't been seen in a decade?"

"She has a valid point," Ruby said.

Either the police had to arrive or I had to escape my house and find safety. "Did Colin even cheat on you, Amy? Or did you make all that up as well to make him sound like a horrible person?"

"Yes. Yes, he did. I was going to wait to get rid of him until after we were married. Have him disappear on our honeymoon or something like that. Maybe a snorkeling accident? Or he'd just... vanish."

I had seen stories like that on the news, of grooms just suddenly disappearing while honeymooning on some isolated, foreign island. The tales had left me pondering many questions. Had he run away? Had something horrible happened to him—like a scuba accident? Now I wondered if the bride had been responsible in most cases.

"But then I realized I had to deal with Jessica," Amy said, shaking her head. "She's been such a pain. Colin's infidelity brought up the perfect opportunity to not only get him out of the way, but also his sister. It's not like everyone knew they were trying to repair their relationship. As far as every relative was concerned, Jessica was still on drugs and had disappeared to wherever drug addicts go. No one knew she was living clean in Prescott!"

Which was only a quick drive away from Sedona. Adam had said the police believed she'd driven into town when she'd discovered her brother would be in Sedona, and then murdered him to inherit the family fortune. But she hadn't. Amy had just made it seem that way.

"You murdered your fiancé," I muttered. "That has to be a new low."

"But I didn't kill him, Bernie," she said sweetly.

I furrowed my brow. "Then who did?"

"You know, I chose to stay here because you minded your own business last time we were in town. Now here you are, sticking your nose in places it doesn't belong. It's all very frustrating to me."

"If you didn't kill him, who did?" I asked again.

"I did."

Spinning around, I found Cathy a few feet behind me. I narrowed my gaze on her, recalling when she first arrived, which had been *after* the murder. "You weren't even in town. You said you couldn't find anyone to cover your shift and you left Phoenix in the early morning hours."

"Holy cow!" Ruby yelled. "I didn't see

that one coming, and I should have! Rule number one-hundred-and-five of life: never trust the quiet ones!"

Cathy shrugged. "I lied to cover my tracks. When Amy needs me, I come. That's what friends do."

I glanced from the kitchen to the living room. Each woman stood in the way of me escaping the house and it suddenly felt as if the walls were closing in. "You two worked together?" I turned to Cathy. "And what do you get out of it?"

She sighed and shrugged, as if sticking a knife in a man's chest was like running a grocery store errand for someone. "Well, I made sure an immature piece of turd got what he deserved, and Amy has promised that I'd be compensated for my troubles. She's my friend, Bernie. I'd do anything for her."

They'd hatched the plan together and pulled it off almost flawlessly. Amy playing the grieving fiancée while Cathy was her best friend, her rock when the bride was destroyed by the killing of the love of her life.

Cathy and I weren't that much different.

A friend had been in need and we had both stepped in to ease our friend's worries. I had broken into my boyfriend's house and gotten caught; she'd killed her friend's fiancé. Granted, Cathy went farther than I could have ever imagined and her logic was far more twisted than mine, but we'd both committed crimes in the name of friendship.

"You've been very good to us," Cathy said. "Even provided us with the murder weapon."

I remembered Darla saying the knife that had been used to kill Colin matched her set... and the one she'd given me for Christmas the prior year. Except I hadn't even noticed I had one missing.

The kitchen was my least favorite place in the house. As a terrible cook, I didn't like spending time in there. If I *had* noticed my butcher block had a knife missing, I would have assumed that I accidently stuck it in a drawer while emptying the dishwasher— not that it had been scooped up by a psychotic murderer. Some sleuth I was.

"I took it before I left the house to go

meet him," Amy explained. "Then gave it to Cathy."

How did I not see all this before? Perhaps because Amy was always crying? Because Cathy always acted like the concerned friend? They had been so emotional and hadn't acted like killers at all. Well, not like my definition of what a killer should be.

"So, I'm asking you again," Amy said. "Where's the bag?"

Not the right question. Where were *the police?!*

"What are you going to do then?" I asked. "Take your bloody disguise and make a run for it?"

"Is it really any of your business?" Amy asked, slowly walking toward me. "Where is it?"

Fear constricted my chest like a vise as sweat dotted my brow. Visions of being tossed over a stairwell came to mind, as did the anxiety from the memory. My breath sawed when I glanced from Amy to Cathy. I began to spiral in panic.

"Mayday! Mayday!" Ruby shouted. "I can see you're about to crumble, Bernie! Don't let the bad stuff win! Fight like a girl! You've been training for this!"

Cathy grabbed me from behind as Amy lunged at me. I froze for a second, but then something within me snapped. I leaned back against Cathy, raised my legs and kicked Amy in the face causing her to stumble away from me.

My weight shift sent Cathy and me to the floor. As we landed, she grunted and her breath caressed the back of my neck. I rolled away from her, scrambling to my feet, then kicked her in the ribs just to make sure the wind had been knocked out of her.

Amy slowly stood and ran at me, screaming at the top of her lungs, her hair flying behind her like a cape, her mouth open and eyes wide. She scared the bejeezus out of me, but I had to keep my head in the game. Stepping to the side right before she plowed into me caused her to run into the dining room table. I quickly brought my elbow down right between her shoulder blades as hard as I could.

"That's my girl!" Ruby yelled. "Kick the snot out of these two!"

I glanced over to find her shadowboxing, her purple mumu swirling around her scrawny calves. If I hadn't been so frightened, I may have laughed.

Turning, I made a mad dash for the door. When I flung it open, I found Jezebel.

"What's wrong, Bernie?" she asked as I brushed past her.

Placing my hands on my knees, I sucked in air as if I'd been without for hours. I raised my arm and pointed inside, gasping out between each breath, "The... killer. They're... inside."

"*They?*"

I nodded. "Amy and Cathy."

"Did you call the cops?"

"Y-yes."

"Are they armed?"

I shook my head.

"Did they try to hurt you?"

Standing upright, I placed my hands on my hips. "Yes."

"Wait here," Jezebel said, cracking her knuckles. "I'll take care of business until the cops arrive."

She stepped inside and shut the door as I

sunk to my knees on my walkway. Should I go in and help her *take care of business?* Whatever that meant? Jezebel yelled something I couldn't understand and before I could make a decision about going back inside the house, a police car pulled up. A deputy I didn't know exited the cruiser. Tears streamed down my cheeks from the stark fear of my ordeal and anger at Adam. He hadn't believed a word I said.

"I was told to come to this address?" the man said. With his red hair and smattering of freckles across the bridge of his nose, he didn't look a day older than fifteen. Must be new.

"Yes. The sheriff has the wrong person in custody for the murder at the hotel. The true killers are inside."

His eyes widened as his stare bounced from the door back to me.

"They confessed to me. I found evidence... a bloody sweatshirt and a long black wig. They used the items to make everyone think Colin's sister had killed him."

"Where's this evidence?"

"Inside. I hid it."

"And the killers? What are they doing in there?" He pointed to the house.

"They're being... subdued," I said, unsure exactly what Jezebel was up to.

"By who?"

"The owner of Tip 'Em Back."

"Jezebel?"

"Yes."

The deputy shook his head and smiled. "I feel bad for those two. I've seen that woman in a few fistfights. Let's just say she never loses."

I followed him into the house to find Amy and Cathy sitting on the living room couch, both with tears rolling down their faces. Jezebel stood in front of them with her arms crossed over her chest, her legs wide. Ruby was next to her, mirroring her stance. Jezebel gave off an air of... toughness. Ruby, on the other hand, simply looked ridiculous.

I noted Amy's eye had turned red and swelled. Had I done that when I kicked her in the face, or was the injury courtesy of Jezebel's fist?

"Aren't you Colin Victory's fiancée?" the deputy asked, pointing at Amy.

"She's a cold-blooded killer!" Ruby yelled.

"Yes!" Amy wailed. "I didn't kill anyone! The love of my life is gone and I'm being treated like a criminal!"

"Give it a rest, Amy," I said. Now that I was safe, anger coursed through me. If the cop hadn't been standing next to me, I may have hit her myself. "You confessed."

Amy glared at me then glanced at Cathy. Jumping from the couch, she pointed at her. "She did it! She killed Colin! She was in love with him and when he told her he loved me, she killed him for revenge!"

"Don't you dare, Amy!" Cathy screamed. "You aren't going to throw me under the bus like that!"

"Sit your scrawny butt down," Jezebel said, stepping in front of Amy and pointing to the couch.

"Yeah! Plant it on the cushion, skinny-minny!" Ruby said.

Amy did as instructed while the deputy called for backup. I listened intently. Would it be Adam? I sincerely hoped not. I didn't want to see him.

Another police cruiser arrived a few minutes later. Relief swept through me as Sheriff Walker breezed into the house.

"Well, hello, Brucey-Boy," Ruby said, sidling up next to him. "Aren't you looking official today?"

Walker glanced at me and shook his head, as if he couldn't believe I'd found myself in the middle of another murder investigation. He wasn't the only one.

Once Amy and Cathy were cuffed and he read their rights, he strode over to me. "My deputy said you have evidence?"

I nodded. "It's hidden in my bedroom." He followed me through the dining room and kitchen and waited by the door while I retrieved the bag from my closet. "Here," I said, handing it to him. "It was out in the garbage can. I found it by accident."

He opened it and glanced inside. "Good thing you did. We thought we had the case all wrapped up based on the hotel security footage."

"They did that on purpose to make everyone think it was Jessica."

"Those two almost pulled it off," the sheriff said, shaking his head. "Evil in their hearts." He glanced around the bedroom for a moment as Ruby appeared directly in front of him.

"Bruce and I had some good times in this bedroom. I bet he's reliving each one right now."

I sighed and closed my eyes, forcing my imagination not to conjure up visions I wouldn't be able to unsee.

"It's a good thing they made weed legal, Bernie," Walker said, turning to me. "If not, I'd have to take you in." With Ruby standing directly in front of him, he'd be enveloped in marijuana and lavender.

I sighed and simply smiled. It was pointless to tell him he was smelling my grandmother's ghost.

"We'll clear out," he continued. "You'll need to come down for a statement."

"Can I just give it here?" I asked. "Maybe have the deputy take it from me? It's been a really rough day."

In reality, I didn't want to chance running into Adam.

"Sure, we can do that. I'll take the two girls in and leave him here with you."

I didn't bother to point out they were women. Murderous women.

When we returned to the living room, Jezebel walked over. "You okay?"

"Yes. Why did you come here?" If she hadn't, who knows what would have happened? Cathy and Amy could have escaped. Or chased me down and killed me.

"We had class today and I called a bunch of times. When you didn't answer, I had to come see what was up."

Between being dumped by Adam, discovering the killer's disguise, and dealing with Amy and Cathy, I'd completely forgotten about my self-defense class. Thankfully, being tossed around by Jezebel had come in handy. "I'm so glad you did," I said. "Thank you."

"Of course. You've got to talk to the police, so I'm outta here. I'll check in with you later." Then she leaned in and added in a whisper, "Tell Ruby that if her brain was dynamite, there wouldn't be enough to blow her hat off."

I burst out laughing as I searched for my ghost. The deputy stared at me as Jezebel walked out of the house with a wave.

"Miss Maxwell? Can we get to the interview?" he asked.

"Of course," I said, wiping my eyes.

We sat down on the couches opposite each other.

"Now tell me exactly what happened."

I took a deep breath. Relief sweeping through me, I began to tell my tale.

EPILOGUE

Two months later

"*T*his is ridiculous!" I shouted at Ruby. We stood in the kitchen and I waved the letter from the IRS above my head. "How in the world am I supposed to pay this?"

Ruby shrugged. "I don't know, honey. I wish I hadn't spent all my money like a drunken sailor so I had more to leave you."

I looked down at the tax bill and groaned. "What am I going to do?"

"Well, first, I think you should start taking cash. You don't have to report cash to Uncle Sam."

"Yes, you do!" I said. "It's illegal not to!"

"Well, it could also be classified as keeping what's yours, but you and I tend to look at things a little differently."

I rolled my eyes. "Do you have any advice that falls into the legal realm?"

"Perhaps you should look into restructuring your business. That may offer some tax benefits."

"Where would I get that done?"

"I knew a lawyer while I was still kicking. Stanley Jones III. Nice guy. He did some work for me."

"Like what?" I asked, picking up my phone and typing in his name.

"A little of this, a little of that. Just tell him who you are and he'll see you right away."

I found the phone number and dialed. As I waited for an answer, I wondered if Ruby had slept with the man or if they'd truly had a working association.

"Did you have a relationship with him?" I asked.

She shook her head and tossed her gray ponytail over her shoulder. "Heck, no.

Stanley was married and I didn't sleep with married men. He also fell out of the ugly tree at birth and hit every branch on the way down. Not my type. Nice guy though."

"Stanley Jones and Associates," the pleasant woman's voice answered. "This is Penny."

"Hi, Penny. My name's Bernadette Maxwell. I need some help restructuring my business for tax purposes, and I was told Mr. Jones could help me."

"Of course. Let me see when we can get you in. Please hold."

Elevator music played as I sighed.

"Drop my name," Ruby said. "Penny knows me well. I bet you'd have an appointment this afternoon or tomorrow."

Penny came back on the line. "Does next week work for you?"

I glanced at Ruby, hating the idea of waiting that long for a meeting. With this tax bill hanging over my head, my anxiety would be through the roof and all I'd do is worry about how I would pay the bill. I needed to act. "Well, I was hoping to get in a little earlier if possible. I found his name in my grandmother's papers. Ruby—"

"You're Ruby's granddaughter?" Penny asked.

"Yes."

"Hold please."

I narrowed my gaze at my ghost. "What's the deal with you and this office?"

She shrugged. "I brought them a lot of business."

"Bernadette?" Penny said.

"You can call me Bernie."

"Well, Bernie, Mr. Jones has an opening today at two. Will that work for you?"

"Yes. Thank you. I'll see you then."

Hanging up the phone, I narrowed my gaze at Ruby. It shouldn't surprise me that dropping my grandmother's name would open doors in this town. She'd been sort of a legend, especially in the sheriff's office. "I'd love to know the story on why your name gets me a same day appointment."

"I told you, I brought him a lot of business. Jezzy's grandma, Janis, the guy who used to own Plates of Pancakes when it was around... I used to be a big deal in this town, Bernie."

"Okay. Well, I have to be there at two."

"Can't wait to see old Stanley again!" Ruby said.

RUBY and I drove to a house that had been converted into a small office building. She spun around in circles next to me as I strode up the sidewalk. With Thanksgiving just two weeks away, the air felt downright wintery, and I pulled my coat tighter around me. People always associated Arizona with extreme heat, but there were those of us up in the mountains who experienced snow during the winter months while those in the valley finally emerged from their long, hot summer to tepid temperatures.

When I arrived at the front door, I knocked.

"No need to do that," Ruby said. "Just waltz right in. It's an office."

Placing my hand on the knob, I turned it

and pushed the door open. I found an empty desk and three blue office chairs in the reception area that used to be a living room. The walls had been painted eggshell white and decorated with pictures of the Arizona skies during a monsoon: lightning, rolling black clouds, torrential rains and dust storms.

"These are amazing photos," I murmured as Ruby and I studied them.

"Janis took a lot of these," Ruby said. "We used to grab a bottle of tequila and go out to the desert during the storms so she could snap pictures."

I wouldn't be able to take such beautiful photos sober, let alone after drinking tequila. It seemed like Mother Nature had posed for each picture, lining up her lightning rods over the cliffs or swirling her clouds into perfect mosaics of black and grey. "I'm impressed. If Janis took these, what are they doing here?"

"Stanley did some legal work for the bar and this was how she paid him. She could get a couple hundred Benjis per picture."

"Seriously?"

"Yup." She turned to face the reception

area. "You better pound on a desk or something to get someone out here. If I remember right, Penny's got a bit of a hearing problem."

"Hello?" I called.

"You know, I've been thinking about you and Adam," she said.

"There's nothing to think about," I muttered. "I don't want to talk about it."

I had successfully avoided him for the past month. Not that he'd come looking for me, but we hadn't seen each other. Slowly, my heart had begun to mend. I still regretted breaking into his condo, but I was also happy to see Darla doing so well. She'd opened the diner and she and Jack were spending a lot of time together.

"Well, I want to go see Ned."

"I'm sorry, Ruby," I whispered, hoping no one was eavesdropping. "I can't do that."

"You could stand outside Adam's door while I say hello," she replied. "I miss that crochety old cowboy and imagine how lonely he is!"

Ned had been alone for decades and he said he preferred the quiet. I didn't worry about him not having Ruby around in the least bit. He might be enjoying his peace.

Crossing my arms over my chest, I shook my head. No way was I going to get within a mile of Adam's condo.

"I think it would—"

"Just stop right there," I hissed, glancing down the hallway to make sure no one was coming. "You can't talk me into this, so stop trying."

Ruby grumbled something about bad attitudes, then turned back to the pictures.

"Hello?" I called again.

"I'm going to head back and see what's going on," she said. "It's better than hanging with Miss No-Can-Do."

Since she couldn't go more than fifteen feet from me outside our house, I stood at the mouth of the hallway so she could search as much of the building as possible. What I longed to do was take off toward the front door and have our tether snap her back behind me simply because she hated when I did it. Yet, this was no place to start a fight and I did need to find out how to lower my dang taxes.

"No one in the kitchen," she said as she appeared from the entrance to the left. Moving across the hall, she ghosted through a door.

"Looks like he's got himself a partner," Ruby said after returning to the hallway. "That room used to be storage, but now there's a messy desk and some file cabinets." She motioned me to follow her. "Come down here a ways. I'm at the end of my leash."

I took a few steps and glanced around the corner at the empty kitchen. The coffee pot was on and dirty dishes littered the sink.

"Come on, Bernie!" Ruby said. "You're holding me back!"

As I inched up the hallway, I passed a bathroom door also on my left. Then another room to the right which held a large wooden table and some filing cabinets—a meeting room of sorts.

More monsoon pictures decorated the walls detailing the fury of Mother Nature. Angry black clouds, fingers of lightning bolts, streams of torrential rains where hard, desert land had been only moments before. My heart thumped loudly as I stared at one particularly fierce photo and it suddenly felt as if that storm was coming alive right in this small home.

"What's your problem?" Ruby chided. "We still have to check this back room. We'll probably find old Stanley in here on the toilet or something."

I glanced back at the front door. Where had everyone gone? At two o'clock in the afternoon on a Wednesday, I expected a lawyer's office to be busy. Where was Penny, the receptionist? And why was the coffee pot on if no one was here?

"I have a bad feeling about this," I whispered. "I think we should leave."

"No. We've got one more room to investigate. I'm sure Stanley just stepped out for a minute or he's in the bathroom. He's even deafer than Penny."

I hesitantly moved closer to the doorway and Ruby was able to slip in. She immediately returned.

"Uh oh," she said. "We have a problem."

"What? What's wrong?"

"The lawyer... he's lifeless. Stanley's dead."

Dear Reader,

I hope you enjoyed the Fiancé is Finished and will consider leaving a review where you purchased it!

Ready for Bernie and Ruby's next adventure? Dive into The Lawyer is Lifeless!

ALSO BY CARLY WINTER

The Tri-Town Murders

Complete Series

Follow newspaper reporter Tilly and her group of fun, quirky friends as they solve murders in a fictional, small town in California.

News and Nectarines

News and Nachos

News and Nutmeg

News and Noodles

Killer Skies Mysteries

Set in 1965, join Patty Briggs, stewardess extraordinaire, as she flies the skies and solves murders with the help of her friends… and one cute FBI agent!

ABOUT THE AUTHOR

Carly Winter is the pen name for a USA Today best-selling and award-winning romance author.

When not writing, she enjoys spending time with her family, reading and enjoying the fantastic Arizona weather (except summer - she doesn't like summer). She does like dogs, wine and chocolate and wishes Christmas happened twice a year.

For more information on her books, please visit: CarlyWinterCozyMysteries.com

www.ingramcontent.com/pod-product-compliance
Lightning Source LLC
Chambersburg PA
CBHW050232110726
47898CB00007B/2119